the further adventures of

SHERLOCK HOLMES

THE STAR OF INDIA

the further adventures of

SHERLOCK HOLMES

THE STAR OF INDIA

CAROLE BUGGÉ

TITAN BOOKS

THE FURTHER ADVENTURES OF SHERLOCK HOLMES:
THE STAR OF INDIA
Print edition ISBN: 9780857681218
E-book edition ISBN: 9780857685414

Published by
Titan Books
A division of Titan Publishing Group Ltd
144 Southwark St
London
SE1 0UP

First edition: August 2011
10 9 8 7 6 5 4 3 2 1

Names, places and incidents are either products of the author's
imagination or used fictitiously. Any resemblance to actual persons, living
or dead (except for satirical purposes), is entirely coincidental.

Visit our website:
www.titanbooks.com

What did you think of this book? We love to hear from our
readers. Please email us at: readerfeedback@titanemail.com,
or write to us at the above address. To receive advance information,
news, competitions, and exclusive Titan offers online, please register
as a member by clicking the 'sign up' button on our website:
www.titanbooks.com

A CIP catalogue record for this title is available from the British Library.

Printed in the USA.

One

I have often remarked upon the moody nature of my friend Sherlock Holmes, so it should have come as no surprise that, when I called upon him on a rainy Saturday in October of 1894, I found him in the sitting room of 221B Baker Street, lying on the couch listlessly tossing darts at the initials V.R., which had been spelled into the wall by bullet holes. Since the death of my second wife, I had taken to calling on Holmes on Saturday afternoons, but it had been several weeks since my last visit.

"Come in!" he barked in response to my knock.

"Ah, it's you, Watson," he said when I entered.

"I didn't see Mrs. Hudson anywhere, so I let myself in," I said, stepping over a pile of newspapers which nearly blocked the door from opening. The thick aroma of Turkish tobacco hung heavily in the air, and a puff of smoke escaped into the hall when I opened the door.

"Well, come in; that is, if you don't mind being horribly bored. Nothing," he said, punctuating the word with a toss of a dart, "nothing of interest is taking place in London—no one of note is trying their wits against the forces of law and order." He sighed and sat up, unfolding his long frame from the sofa. "It is an irony of my profession that when my fellow creatures are enjoying a period of relative peace and quiet, I find myself in the uncomfortable position of wishing that something interesting would happen to spoil it."

"But surely you don't wish—" I said, hanging up my cloak and hat.

"Oh, but I do, Watson; that's the damnable part of it."

He threw another dart, which landed at the base of the V and stuck in a bullet hole. Holmes sighed and lit a cigarette. He was wearing his old mouse-colored dressing gown and looked as though he hadn't shaved—always a bad sign in someone usually so meticulous about his appearance. I was also dismayed to see the stack of newspaper clippings in the corner of the room. When unoccupied with cases, Holmes was in the habit of clipping items from the newspapers, and the size of the pile indicated that it had been some time since he had had a crime to solve. The familiar sitting room, though untidy, was by no means in a shambles the way it often was when Holmes was working. The Persian slipper containing his shag tobacco hung from a nail on the hearth; his test tubes and beakers sat unused upon his makeshift laboratory table.

"Do you mind if I open a window?" I said, coughing. My lungs felt heavy; the acrid smell of stale tobacco was so strong I could taste it on my tongue.

Holmes shrugged. "Go ahead. Frankly, Watson, with Moriarty dead and Colonel Moran behind bars, I am afraid I shall die of boredom," he said, lying back on the couch and blowing a smoke ring into the air. It curled and hung in the lamplight for a moment before dissipating into a thin gray wisp.

I opened the window and inhaled the smells of a London afternoon: the sweat of horses mingled with the aroma of roasting chestnuts, damp clothes, and boiling cabbage. I walked over to the fire which blazed in the grate and rubbed my hands. I had been at my surgery all morning and was cold and tired. It had been an unusually busy week and only now did I realize how exhausted I was. An early influenza epidemic—the first of the season—had forced me to keep long hours. Right now, what I wanted more than anything was a glass of brandy and a good meal.

"My dear fellow—" I began, but Holmes interrupted me.

"Yes, yes, I know!" he said impatiently, springing up from the couch and pacing up and down in front of the hearth. "The sad fact is I often don't hear about a case until some great harm has already been done… and believe me, I do not relish the suffering of others."

"Of course you don't, Holmes—"

"But I must have stimulation!" he cried suddenly, tossing his cigarette into the grate and throwing himself down on his favorite chair in front of the fire. I caught Holmes glancing toward the desk where I knew he kept his cocaine. I felt a chill go through me which even the roaring fire could not warm. I could not bear to see Holmes under the influence of this evil habit, see it destroy his nerves and his health, and yet I knew that he did not take kindly to interference on my part. I decided not to bring up the subject, and tried diversion instead.

"You know, I have some tickets to the concert at the Royal Albert Hall tonight; would you like to come along with me?"

His face brightened slightly. "Sarasate is playing the Saint-Saëns third violin concerto tonight," he said languidly.

"Shall we go?" I said, trying not to sound anxious.

"Well…" he said, looking out at the bleak, bleary day. "Oh, why not?" he cried suddenly, springing up from his chair. "After all, there's no point in moping around here."

With that, he disappeared into his bedroom, and I heard the sound of drawers opening and closing, and the clatter of hangers being flung about. Holmes was a study in contrasts: his moods seemed to range from utterly listless to intensely energetic, with very little in between.

I helped myself to some brandy and sat in my usual chair before the fire while Holmes dressed, listening to the hiss of rain on the street outside. The flames from the fireplace cast a yellow glow about the room, and the brandy was warm on my throat. My eyes fell on the picture of Reichenbach Falls which hung above the mantel, and, once again, a shiver wormed its way up my spine. It was three and a half years since that fateful day in Switzerland when I thought I had lost my friend forever, and yet every detail of that horrid scene remained fresh in my mind: his abandoned walking stick leaning up against the rock, the farewell note so carefully written in Holmes' firm, clear hand. Indeed, the note did such a good job of deceiving me that I never questioned that my friend had fallen to his death over that awful precipice, along with Professor Moriarty. It was a long three years before I found out that I was mistaken, and the months since had an unreal quality about them. I sometimes felt I was dreaming, and that I would awaken to find Holmes was dead after all.

"Do you need to eat first?" he called out from the bedroom.

I was touched by my friend's concern, knowing that for him food was often nothing more than a necessary evil. Though he was known to enjoy a feast at Simpson's, his lean figure attested to his general impatience with the demands of the body. I sometimes thought that one of my functions in our friendship was to keep him from collapsing outright from the extreme demands he often placed upon his constitution.

"Maybe Mrs. Hudson can put a sandwich together for me before we leave," I said.

"Oh, she's visiting her sister in the West Country," he said, appearing from the other room in a starched white shirt and tails.

"That's better, don't you think?" he said with a wink. I knew that Holmes was aware of my concerns, and that he did his best not to alarm me unduly.

Trying not to show how pleased I was, I got my coat and hat.

"What about food for you?" said Holmes as we left, pulling the door of the sitting room closed behind us.

"I'm all right," I answered. "I had a glass of brandy. We can have something afterwards."

And so, within minutes, we were seated in a hansom cab rattling off toward the Royal Albert Hall. The rain had settled into a steady drizzle, and I sat watching the droplets bounce off the cobblestones, looking out at the parade of humanity which trudged through the streets of London.

"Look at that, Watson. All the world's a stage, but London... you know, each and every one of those people out there has a story, and most of them will go untold. It's only the ones who commit acts of greatness—of goodness or villainy—that we will ever hear of, or that posterity will remember. For instance, take that man there," he said, indicating a thin, stringy-limbed fish vendor hawking his wares at the open-air market. "He had a career in the military, met with some success, was disappointed in love, and now he is a fish vendor."

I was about to ask Holmes to explain, but not wanting to interrupt his train of thought, I said nothing. Holmes continued. "Does it haunt him, I wonder, that no one is really very curious about his life, and that a hundred years from now no one will even remember that he lived at all? He will be just one of the millions of untold human stories which walk these streets every day."

"Perhaps his family will remember him," I said.

"Perhaps, but after a while even their curiosity will wane, and traces of his existence will gradually vanish from the face of the earth. No, Watson," he said, leaning back in the cab so that his long, lean face was in the shadows, "immortality does not come to those who live commonplace lives; it is the sole province of the doer of extraordinary deeds."

"People live on in their children," I said.

"Ah, yes, progeny," he replied gloomily. "Well, I suppose there must be some reward for having children, otherwise people wouldn't do it at all."

I smiled; the remark was so typical of Holmes. Though we never spoke of it, I had often wondered if Holmes regretted not having children. My own regrets on the subject sometimes hit me with a sharpness which surprised me.

"I mean, family is all well and fine, if that's what you want," Holmes continued. "But for the majority of mankind, greatness alone results in true immortality. Therefore you have your Caesars, your Napoleons, your Alexanders... do you know they say that Alexander wept when he realized that there were no more worlds to conquer?"

"Yes, I think I heard that," I said drily, not sure I wanted to encourage this train of thought. Holmes closed his eyes, but the muscles on his face were taut as ever, and I imagined him as a young conqueror, astride his horse, weeping because there were no more worlds left to conquer.

The cab arrived at the Royal Albert Hall; we alighted and paid the driver. The rain was falling more heavily now, and a sea of black umbrellas greeted us as we made our way up the front steps. (Holmes hated umbrellas, and in spite of the inclement London weather, rarely carried one.) We ducked and wound our way through the crowd of people, arriving at our seats just as the first strains of Bach drifted up to the balcony.

Holmes sat throughout the entire concert with his eyes closed, fingertips pressed together, in an attitude of complete concentration. I tried to listen to the music, each phrase twisting and turning around itself like the spinning of a web, but I was somewhat distracted. The attractive young woman in front of us was wearing a musky perfume which, for some reason, made my throat constrict, and I spent much of the first half of the concert stifling coughs. Holmes didn't seem to notice, and sat serenely until intermission. Fortunately for me, the young woman did not return to her seat after intermission, and I was able to enjoy the second half of the concert.

On the ride home, Holmes was silent for a long time, and then he said, "It was a true test of friendship, your suffering through that concert, Watson."

"What do you mean?"

"Well, you were evidently having an allergic reaction—to the perfume, I should think; it was rather overwhelming. I myself found it somewhat difficult to breathe until I began practicing a breathing technique which I learned from the Dalai Lama during my sojourn with him."

I laughed. I should have known better than to suppose that anything went unnoticed by Holmes.

"And our little jaunt has had the effect you intended, though not for the reason you might suppose."

"What do you mean?" I said, confused.

"Oh, Watson, do you suppose that I didn't notice your concern over my state of mind? Your suggestion that we take in this concert was such a transparent attempt to divert me! I agreed to go because I was so touched at your concern."

"Well, I'm glad you found it so flattering," I said, feeling a little put out by his superior tone. "But what did you mean when you said that it had the effect I wanted, but not—"

"Ah," he replied. "Well, let me ask you this: did you notice that the young lady with the perfume was not in her seat during the second half of the concert?"

"Of course," I said sulkily. "I was able to breathe during the second half."

"Yes, yes, so you were," he said. "But do you know *why* she was not present?"

"I suppose because she was bored by the music," I said. "Does it matter?"

"Oh, it matters a great deal," said Holmes. "She did not return during the second half because she was unable to do what she had come there to do."

"Oh?" I said, still feeling annoyed at Holmes. "And what was that?"

"To deliver a message."

"A message? What kind of message?"

"One that evidently had some urgency, but that had to be delivered secretly."

I was silent; I tried to remember what I had seen at intermission, and had a vague memory of noticing the young lady in question among the crowd in the lobby at one point, but nothing stuck in my mind. I stared moodily out the window of our cab at the wet, huddled throngs of fellow Londoners slogging through the cobblestone streets. Finally, Holmes broke the silence.

"Didn't it strike you as odd that such an attractive young lady would attend a concert alone?"

"Well, perhaps—"

"And furthermore, that, even though the concert featured a very popular performer, the seat next to her was unoccupied?"

The woman had indeed sat alone, and the aisle seat next to her had remained empty for the duration of the concert.

"Yes, perhaps, but..."

"You see, Watson; you look, but you do not observe. If the first observable facts about our young lady had not raised my interest, the perfume certainly would have."

"The perfume?"

"Yes, the perfume that you yourself noticed because it caused an allergic reaction in your respiratory system."

"What about it?" I said, but instead of answering, Holmes rapped on the roof of the cab to signal to the driver. The man's ruddy face appeared upside down in the window, rain dripping from his cap.

"Yes, sir?"

"Take a right here, please, driver."

"Yes, sir," the man said, and the face disappeared.

We were in the outskirts of Covent Garden, that part of London where costermongers mingled with street hawkers of all sorts: piemen, eel vendors, Irish apple women, and flower girls with bunches of violets.

"Do you think you can put off your dinner just a while longer, Watson?" said Holmes suddenly.

"Certainly. Why?"

"I'm curious about that exotic perfume."

I, too, was curious, and was about to ask Holmes what he had in mind, when he rapped on the roof of the cab again. Once more the driver's sodden face appeared in the window.

"Here, sir?"

"Yes, thank you, this will do."

We disembarked and paid the driver, and Holmes led me through the crowded streets, past baked-potato sellers and greengrocers in blue aprons. The cries of vendors filled the air:

"Fine firm apples! Care to try one, sir?"

"Eels—hot pickled eels!"

"Violets, penny a bunch!"

I wanted to ask Holmes where we were going, but he walked briskly in front of me, his head bent over like a bird dog on a scent. I had no choice but to follow, stepping over cobblestones littered with walnut shells, cabbage leaves, and squashed oranges. We turned onto a little street in the shadow of St. Paul's Church, and then down a narrow alley, leaving the noise and clatter of the market behind us. Holmes stopped in front of a shop which had all the appearance of being boarded up. He rapped sharply on the door with his walking stick, and the sound reverberated through the narrow twisted street. We stood there, rain dripping from our top hats—in my excitement I had left my umbrella in the cab—until a voice called out from deep within the shop.

"Who's there?"

"It's Sherlock Holmes."

There was the sound of something being dragged across a wooden floor, and then the door opened. I had seen many a strange character on my numerous adventures with Holmes, but I was unprepared for the sight which greeted us at the door.

The man's age was impossible to tell; he could have been thirty or eighty. His nose didn't resemble a nose so much as it did a swollen gourd: purple, bumpy, and distended, it dominated a face which, even without it, would have been grotesque. His one good eye was blue—strikingly blue, the color of turquoise—and his other eye was covered by a lump of flesh which protruded from his forehead. His entire face was so misshapen that his mouth was pulled upward in a sort of lopsided grin. His skull was comprised of uneven layers of bumps and lumps; his head was altogether massive and sat upon his spindly body like a pumpkin teetering upon a post. His limbs were underdeveloped, and his spine was so twisted that it was impossible for him to stand up straight. He held the doorjamb with his right hand in order to keep his balance.

I tried my best not to stare at him, but, in spite of my medical training and my experiences with wounded men in the war, I am afraid I did not succeed. Holmes, however, greeted the man with a friendly familiarity.

"Good evening, Mr. Wiggins," he said. "You will forgive me, I hope, for calling at this hour?"

To my surprise the man's voice was as beautiful as his body was hideous.

"Not at all, Mr. Holmes," he said in a smooth, cultivated baritone with just a trace of a foreign accent. "Come right in."

He opened the door wider to admit us into the room. I had another surprise when I saw the interior of his shop, for it bore no resemblance to its crumbling exterior. The place was immaculate: the carefully sanded and swept wooden floors were covered by richly hued handwoven Persian carpets. More amazing to me was the fact that the entire room was taken up by floor-to-ceiling shelves, which were stocked with the most amazing assortment of bottles I had ever seen—all sizes, shapes, and colors imaginable. The heady mixture of scents in the room at once advertised the fact that the bottles contained perfumes. The combination of so many aromas was intoxicating, and I felt absolutely lightheaded as I walked about the room, taking in his collection with open-mouthed admiration.

"May I present my friend and colleague, Dr. Watson," said Holmes. "Watson, this is Jeremiah Wiggins, perfumer extraordinaire."

"Is there any kind of perfume you *don't* carry?" I finally said to our host, swept away by such a dazzling array of bottles.

"What are you looking for?" said a voice behind me, but it wasn't Wiggins—in fact, it wasn't a human voice at all. I turned around: behind the counter which held the cash register, an enormous blue and yellow parrot sat on a perch. The parrot regarded me through one bright orange eye, his head cocked sideways.

"What are you looking for?" he repeated, bobbing up and down on his perch.

"He likes you, Watson," said Holmes, laughing the peculiar dry laugh of his.

"How can you tell?" I said, not sure whether it was a compliment or not.

"See the way he's bobbing up and down?" said Mr. Wiggins. "That means he's excited. Sometimes he bobs like that when he just wants attention or is agitated about something."

"What is he?" I said, "I mean, what kind?"

"He's originally from South America," said Mr. Wiggins, "though I got him from an Indian gentleman of my acquaintance, one of my clients. His name is Bandu, which is Bengali for 'friend.'"

This revelation caused me to wonder even more about our friend's refined manners. He was evidently well educated; was it also possible that he had traveled widely?

Wiggins hobbled over to the parrot and held out a skinny arm to the bird. The parrot hopped from his perch onto Wiggins' hand.

"Peck on the cheek, Bandu," said Wiggins, and the parrot repeated the words after him.

"Peck on the cheek, peck on the cheek," said the bird, and then rubbed the blunt top of his beak against Wiggins' poor deformed cheek.

"He's a great talker," said Wiggins, "and a very fast learner. Bandu gets bored with his old phrases and is always adding new ones. He'll probably be imitating you after you've gone." He stroked the bird's bright feathers. "He's very affectionate, as you can see. He even cries when I leave—which, fortunately for both of us, is not often."

I thought of Wiggins alone in his little shop, surrounded by his perfume bottles and his bird, safe from the curious stares of his fellow creatures; to the bird, he was no different from anyone else.

"I don't know how old he was when I got him, but he may very well outlive me," Wiggins said as he placed the bird back on its perch.

"Yes, they live a long time, don't they?" said Holmes.

I looked at Holmes; he was standing in front of the shelves, studying the bottles. It occurred to me that he was being unusually patient. Exchanging small talk was never his forte, and yet he stood there in Wiggins' shop as though he had all the time in the world. I came to the conclusion that he either felt sorry for the man or simply liked him. As though reading my mind, Wiggins turned to Holmes.

"So, Mr. Holmes, what can I do for you today?" he said, sitting on an intricately carved little stool which sat in front of his counter.

"Well, I've come across a scent that I can't quite identify, and I need your help."

Wiggins smiled, or at least his mouth twisted into its own version of a smile. To my surprise, I found the expression rather charming instead of horrifying. Somehow the man's gentle, refined nature shone through the hideous exterior that a cruel trick of Nature had given him.

"What, Mr. Holmes," he said, crossing his thin arms. "Do you mean to tell me that there exists a scent in London that you can't identify?"

Holmes smiled in response. Now I was certain that rather than feeling sorry for Wiggins, he liked and admired the man.

"I'm afraid so, although I would appreciate it if you didn't broadcast the fact. After all, I do have my reputation to think about."

Wiggins laughed, a deep, gurgling chortle, and rose from the stool. With the help of an elegant ebony cane, he moved to the shelf closest to him.

"Tell me as much as you can," he said.

"Definitely foreign, probably Eastern; musky, with a hint of jasmine—and very expensive."

"Expensive, eh?" said Wiggins. "Well, that narrows it down considerably. Let's see..." he said, and his eyes—or rather, his eye—scanned the shelves in front of him. "I think I can narrow it down to three," he said, reaching for a small, opaque green bottle in front of him. "This is one," he said, placing it on the counter behind him. He returned to the shelves and selected a second bottle, this one larger, with a pale blue color. He placed that one on the counter and then turned to Holmes.

"The third is rather high up," he said with no hint of embarrassment or self-pity, "and I believe you're somewhat taller than I–"

"Certainly," said Holmes, and reached for the bottle indicated. This one was even more striking than the others: It was long and thin, and of a deep ruby-red tint that I had never seen in glass before. Our host uncorked each bottle one by one, with the solemn air of a priest conducting an initiation rite. Holmes sniffed each one in turn with equal seriousness, shaking his head at the first two, but when he came to the elegant ruby-red vial, he cried, "That's it–that's the one!"

"That's the one, that's the one," said the parrot behind us. I turned to look at him. He was dancing on his perch, ducking his head up and down and hopping from one foot to the other.

"I told you he's a fast learner," said Wiggins, smiling. "Well, Mr. Holmes, your friend–whoever she is–has expensive taste. You were right when you said that this perfume is dear; what you didn't know is that it is virtually unaffordable for everyone but the wealthiest. It is indeed Eastern–Indian, to be exact. There is indeed a hint of jasmine in it, but the ingredient which makes it so expensive is saffron." He held the bottle out toward me. "See, Dr. Watson, if you can't detect the faint aroma of saffron."

I placed my face above the lid of the bottle, not too close, and inhaled the ineffable sweetness and delicacy of saffron, with its evocation of balmy Indian nights. To my surprise, instead of my earlier allergic reaction, suddenly I was transported for a moment to my younger days as a soldier stationed in the Indian countryside. I had a vision of sitting with my comrades around a table of cards, with a sweet Indian girl at my side, her dark almond eyes smiling into mine as I played cards with my companions.

"Are you quite all right, Watson?" Holmes' sharp voice jerked me out of my reverie.

"Oh, yes, I'm fine; I just—"

"You were experiencing a memory," said Wiggins, smiling. "Yes, perfume can do that to you, especially one of this quality, which seems to contain within it all the scents of one's youth. I believe Mr. Holmes once told me you were stationed in India for a while."

"Yes, I was."

"I myself was born in Calcutta."

"Really?"

"Yes; my father was British, but my mother was Indian."

"I see."

"So this scent is as evocative for you as it is for me," Wiggins said with a lopsided smile.

"Yes; it's not as musky here as it was in the concert hall. When I first smelled it, I seemed to have quite an allergic reaction, but now it's quite pleasant."

"Ah, yes; that is typical of really good perfumes. They merge with the scent of the wearer and take on a different identity with each person."

"Perhaps it was the woman you were allergic to, Watson," Holmes said, smiling.

"That's your department, Holmes," I shot back, "being allergic to women."

"Not allergic, Watson—just distrustful," Holmes corrected me.

"Well, allergies can come and go," Wiggins said cheerfully. "You must know that, being a medical man, Dr. Watson."

"Indeed I do; they are most mysterious."

"Just like women," added Wiggins, with a wink at Holmes.

I had to agree with Wiggins—and particularly mysterious was the young woman at the concert with the musky scent. I wondered about her—who she was, what she was doing at the concert, and why Holmes was so interested in her. But Holmes was already moving toward the door.

"Well, I congratulate you, Mr. Wiggins; once again, you have proved invaluable to me," he said. "What is the name of the scent in question?"

"Golden Nights," said Wiggins. "Believe me when I tell you it costs a king's ransom to buy."

"I would never doubt you, my friend," said Holmes, grasping the man's shoulder affectionately. "Take care of yourself. Here is a little contribution to your research," he added, slipping a few bills into Wiggins' jacket pocket.

"That really isn't necessary," said Wiggins. "It's always a pleasure to be of service to you, Mr. Holmes."

"Take it on my account," Holmes urged. "It will make me feel better."

"Very well; thank you," our host said with a simple dignity.

"Oh, just one last question," said Holmes. "Do any of your clients order this particular scent?"

Wiggins smiled, and again I was struck by the sweetness of the man's nature.

"I'm afraid most of my 'clients,' as you so kindly put it, can't afford a scent like this one. I haven't sold any of this particular scent for years. No, I'm afraid I have that one, as I have most of these," he said, indicating the rows of bottles, "simply for my own amusement. Some I even manufacture myself. Next time you must let me show you my new laboratory equipment."

"I would be delighted," said Holmes, and once again we stepped out into the night.

It was a shock to stand once again in the rain-slicked street after the warm gentility of Mr. Wiggins' shop. We pulled our collars up around our ears and headed back down the alley in search of a cab.

* * *

Before long I was snugly ensconced in the sitting room at Baker Street, sipping brandy and watching the storm as it gathered strength outside, while Holmes rummaged around downstairs for something to eat. I watched as the rain swept in sheets across the deserted streets; only the hardiest of souls would venture out on a night like this. Even the usual procession of hansom cabs had disappeared, leaving the bare cobblestones to receive the brunt of the storm's fury.

Holmes appeared at the door holding a joint of beef in one hand and a loaf of bread in the other.

"Success!" he cried cheerfully. "Good old Mrs. Hudson, reliable to the last."

"That's a strange thing to say. You make it sound as if she had died."

"Hmmm, you're right. I don't know why I said that," he replied, setting the food on the sideboard. "Cornwall may be a form of purgatory, but it isn't quite death, I suppose. I think you had better stay here tonight," he added, drawing the curtains on the tempest outside.

"Thank you, I will," I said, carving myself a large slice of roast beef. As the flu epidemic was finally showing signs of slowing down, I had left my surgery in the care of a colleague for a few days so that I could get some much-needed rest. It was pleasant to be once again in my old digs, sharing brandy with Holmes in front of the fire. His black mood of earlier had lightened and he was in a talkative mood.

"Nature is often a cruel mistress, Watson," he said meditatively, gazing into his brandy glass as the fire crackled and sparked in the grate.

"What do you mean?"

"Well," said Holmes, "it strikes me as terribly cruel that a prince of a man like Wiggins should have been saddled with such a pathetic and repulsive body, whilst spiritually repulsive men often are blessed with the handsomest of figures. Take the odious Baron Gruner, for example. Do you remember him?"

"Remember him!" I exclaimed. "How could I forget him; his henchmen nearly beat you to death. I'll never forget the day I saw the newspaper which carried the report of the attack on you; I thought my heart had stopped—"

Holmes dismissed the memory with a wave of his hand.

"That was a mere trifle compared to the way the baron treated women. A truly venomous snake, that one—and yet Nature gave him the face and figure of a god."

"Well, he got what was coming to him; he was horribly disfigured by the acid which Kitty threw in his face. There was a strange justice in his fate after all."

"True, but by the hand of a woman, not Nature."

I laughed. "Holmes, you know nothing about women if you separate them from Nature—"

Holmes chuckled. "Perhaps you're right... I just regret that a man like Wiggins has to spend his life in such a body. He doesn't deserve such a fate."

"I think I have read of a case such as his in my medical textbooks. A certain John Merrick had a similar disease, and became quite famous after he became the special patient of a London physician."

"Yes, yes; Wiggins has often spoken of Merrick, or the Elephant Man, as he was called, and wished he could meet him. Wiggins himself has had quite a life. I shall tell you about him one day—I count him as one of the many treasures London has to offer the curious adventurer."

"Who are his clients?"

Holmes smiled. "Mostly 'fancy women,' as they are so delicately called. They go to Wiggins for their ounce or two of cologne, because he gives them a good price. More importantly, he treats them with respect."

"I see."

"Oh, Watson, don't look so scandalized! The women themselves aren't evil—the real evil lies in society. It's shameful that conditions are such that a woman has to trade her virtue for a few coins and then be vilified in the process."

I got up and put some more wood on the fire. The log was damp, and smoked and popped when I lowered it onto the flames. I picked up the poker and jabbed at it a bit. Finally, however, I could contain myself no longer.

"Well, Holmes, are you going to tell me about the young woman at the Albert Hall now, or am I going to have to remain in ignorance until you are quite ready to divulge your secrets?"

Holmes laughed. "Secrets? I have no secrets from you, Watson. There are only plain facts, which you yourself could have deduced if you had bothered to observe what I did."

"And exactly what did you observe?"

"Let's start with what you observed, Watson. You noticed the young lady, the empty seat, and the strong perfume, correct?"

"Yes."

"Anything else?"

I tried hard to remember what I had noticed at the concert, but everything was already becoming faint in my mind, blunted by the brandy, the fire, and the lateness of the hour.

"All right, Watson, I'll help. First, the young lady. What did you make of her?"

I never saw her face clearly, only from a side angle, but I had a vague memory of what she wore, a burgundy brocade dress—fashionable enough, but not of the most expensive cut.

"Well, she was well dressed, but not richly dressed."

"Excellent. So now we may surmise she did not buy herself the very expensive perfume which she wore, but that it was given to her as a gift."

"Yes, I suppose that's a reasonable conclusion."

"Was she married?"

"Uh... no, I shouldn't think so."

"Why not?"

"Well, she was alone—"

"Oh, come, Watson; there is no mystery to this one! She wasn't wearing a wedding ring."

I was tired of Holmes' attempt to educate me; I found his use of the Socratic method on this occasion irritating.

"Look, Holmes," I said, "you might as well face that you won't turn me into a reasoning machine such as yourself."

"Very well," he said, shrugging. "Her agitated state of mind was clear to me when I saw her standing by her seat, craning her neck to look around, as though she were expecting to see someone. She remained standing until the moment the lights went down, and then she took her seat for the first half of the concert, leaving, as we both noticed, during the interval. She left so hastily, in fact, that she left these." And with that Holmes produced from his pocket a pair of cream-colored kid gloves.

"She left without her gloves? Why would she do that, I wonder?" I said, examining them. They were of good quality, quite new, and exuded a faint odour of Golden Nights.

"She left without them because she had other more important things to think about," said Holmes, lighting his pipe, "and I can't help wondering what they were."

"Well, I for one am going to bed," I said. "It's late."

"Go ahead, Watson; I'll follow later."

Holmes evidently saw me glance at the desk drawer which contained the dreaded needle, because he smiled. "Don't worry,

Watson; I promise you I shall take nothing stronger than shag tobacco tonight."

I waved my hand at the blue mist of smoke which hung in the air.

"You might cut down a bit on that as well, you know."

Holmes shook his head.

"One vice at a time, Watson."

I went upstairs. I was so tired that I fell upon the bed immediately, only to wake up shivering in the middle of the night. I crept downstairs to see if Holmes had retired. He had not, and was sitting in the same position in which I had left him, his head wreathed in smoke, gazing out the window. Not wanting him to see me, I said nothing and tiptoed back upstairs. The last image in my mind as I fell asleep was of Holmes, seated in his chair, his sharp profile surrounded in smoke which dispersed the yellow lamplight around his head like a halo.

Two

I slept like the dead that night, dreaming of rows and rows of shelves covered with mysterious bottles. I was looking for something in the bottles, but I could not find whatever it was I wanted. I kept dropping bottles to the floor and breaking them. Instead of perfume, they contained acid—like the acid which had so horribly disfigured Baron Gruner's face. Each time a bottle dropped to the floor, it ate a little more of the floorboards away, until finally I was standing on a tiny piece of wood. I awoke, covered in sweat, with that strange sense of relief one always has when a bad dream proves not to be real after all.

When I finally came down to breakfast, it was late and Holmes was already seated at the table. It was evident from his red-rimmed eyes and haggard face that he had not slept, and yet he greeted me cheerfully.

"Ah, Watson, you're just in time to try my own recreation of Mrs. Hudson's famed Scotch eggs," he said, lifting the lid of a silver chafing dish.

I peered dubiously into the dish, expecting untold horrors, but to my surprise the contents did look amazingly like Mrs. Hudson's admirable version of the Scottish delicacy. I spooned some onto my plate.

"Well, what do you think; will it pass muster?" said Holmes, leaning back and lighting a cigarette. The smoke rose and curled around his face, which looked almost gray in the thin morning light. "Try to be kind; I spent a good part of the morning working at it. This may come as a surprise to you, but lately I find cooking almost as calming as smoking when the mind is engaged upon a problem."

"Not bad, not bad at all," I said, tasting it. In truth it wasn't bad, though it lacked the magic touch of Mrs. Hudson's talent.

"Well, you're very kind to say so," said Holmes. "Personally, I find it lacks something–it has the form without the substance, or something to that effect. Never mind; it'll stick to your ribs, and that's what counts on a day like today."

I looked outside. Holmes was right. It was the kind of gray, blustery day that London is famous for, the kind of weather that cuts right through your clothes and chills your bones.

"I hate to rush you, Watson, but we shall have a visitor before the morning is out," Holmes said.

"A visitor?" I said, my mouth full of Scotch egg. "What sort of visitor?"

"Oh, you'll see soon enough."

I sometimes thought one of Holmes' chief pleasures in solving what he called his "little problems" was keeping me in the dark as long as possible. Then, like a theatrical impresario, he would draw aside the curtain and enjoy the astonished gasps of his audience as he revealed in an instant the results of his labors. Fortunately for him, I was usually content enough to play my role, and I certainly was an appreciative audience.

Now, as if on cue, the front bell rang.

"Aha, she is early!" he said, and dashed out of the room. I took a sip of coffee and then settled on the couch to see who this mysterious visitor might be. I didn't have long to wait: within seconds, the pungent odour of Golden Nights wafted up the staircase and in through the open door of the sitting room. A few moments later, Holmes entered the room with the young lady in tow.

"Watson, may I introduce Miss Violet Merriweather; Miss Merriweather, this is my friend and colleague, Dr. John Watson."

"How do you do?" she said in a low and pleasing mezzo.

"Pleased to meet you," I said, and in fact it was a pleasure to be introduced to such an attractive young woman. I have often marveled at Holmes' imperviousness to feminine charms, considering some of the women who have graced the sitting room of 221B Baker Street. This particular young woman had large brown eyes, smooth black hair, and olive skin so lustrous that it shone in the lamplight. She wore a yellow linen dress and a cloak to match; though not showy, both suited her perfectly. I was sorry that I had not paid more attention to her during the concert at the Royal Albert.

"Please sit down, Miss Merriweather," Holmes said smoothly, indicating a chair by the fire.

"Thank you," said our guest, and sat with a delicate grace which made me wonder about her breeding. Her manners and gentility were of the highest refinement, and yet her clothes, while respectable, were not of the first order.

"I believe these are your gloves?" said Holmes, holding out the kid gloves which our visitor had so carelessly left behind the previous evening.

"Yes!" she cried, rising slightly from her chair. "I thought I would never see them again. Thank you so much for retrieving them for me!"

She took the gloves from Holmes and handled them lovingly, as though they were a lost kitten. She looked up at Holmes.

"Please allow me to offer you a small reward—"

Holmes shook his head.

"Certainly not," he said. "It was my pleasure to return them... however, there is one question which you could answer for me."

"Certainly. What is it?"

"I was intrigued by your perfume," said Holmes, "and I wonder if you could tell me where I could find some."

To my surprise, the lady blushed and coughed delicately into her handkerchief.

"It—it was... a gift," she said in a tone which indicated a reluctance to speak about it.

"Ah, I see," said Holmes. "And the gentleman in question— you don't know where he purchased it?"

"No, I'm afraid not," she replied, still blushing, her eyes averted.

"Ah, I see," said Holmes. "I will inquire no further in the matter, madame. I am sorry if I have caused you any discomfort."

"Oh, there is no need to apologize," she answered quickly. "The gentleman in question is—dead, I'm afraid." She was a very bad liar, and this time I was the one who blushed.

But Holmes did not bat an eye. "I see," he said gravely. "I'm very sorry."

"Oh—thank you," she said, sounding surprised that her lie had been accepted. "Well, I'm afraid I must be going," she said, rising from her chair. "Thank you again for your kindness."

"My pleasure," said Holmes, escorting her to the door. "I was happy to be of some small service. And," he said, holding the door open, "please let me know if I can be of any assistance in the present matter which is troubling you."

I had to hand it to Holmes; this stopped Miss Merriweather in her tracks.

"Why, I–I have no idea what you're referring to," she said finally, and it was painfully clear that she knew exactly what he meant. I wondered how much Holmes actually knew and to what extent he was fishing.

"Never mind, Miss Merriweather. I ask nothing except that you consider turning to me when you feel the need for some assistance."

"Well, if I ever need assistance, as you call it, I shall certainly–I mean, all of London knows who you are, Mr. Holmes, and I am no exception."

"Yes, well, that is all I ask. Good day, Miss Merriweather."

"Good day. Good day, Dr. Watson."

"Good day."

She left in a swirl of skirts, leaving a trace of Golden Nights behind her. Holmes closed the door and turned to me, his eyes twinkling, all trace of his former fatigue gone. His lean body shimmered with energy.

"Well, Watson, what do you think of our visitor?"

"She's very attractive–"

"Yes, yes, I know; always the eye for feminine beauty," he said impatiently, cutting me off. "I mean, what do you *think* of her, not what you *feel!*"

"Well, she was obviously lying."

"Wasn't she, though?" he said with relish. "And very badly too. She's not accustomed to lying, Watson, and she's not accustomed to the life she's leading. There's more to her than meets the eye, Watson, mark my words!"

"But how did you know she's in trouble?"

"Well, the gloves were the first indication that all was not well–"

"How did she know you had them, by the way?"

Holmes shrugged. "I sent a message to the Royal Albert Hall early this morning that, if a young lady came to inquire for a pair of cream-colored kid gloves, she could find them at this address."

"Ah–but how did you know she would come today?"

"The gloves themselves told me."

"But how—?"

"Consider, Watson. A certain young lady is given a pair of very expensive gloves by a certain young man. The gloves are much finer than anything she has in her wardrobe. However, the next time she sees him, she is not wearing the gloves. Now, what young man would not become extremely suspicious under such circumstances? Therefore, when she lost the gloves she had to retrieve them as soon as possible."

"But how did you know they were a gift?"

"As I said, they were of much finer quality than the rest of her attire—not the kind of thing that a respectable, but by no means wealthy, young lady could afford for herself. No, I was fairly certain they were a gift—and quite new, at that. Nothing soils so quickly as cream-colored leather, and yet these gloves were spotless."

"So she is a young lady who is seeing a man who is considerably wealthier than she is. Surely there's nothing sinister in that?"

"Perhaps not, Watson; perhaps not. We shall see."

Just then we were interrupted by the sound of the front bell, followed by a boy's voice calling Holmes by name. Holmes went to the window, opened it, and shouted down into the street.

"Yes, what is it?"

"Telegram for Mr. Sherlock Holmes!"

Before I could speak, Holmes was out the door and down the steps. I saw him conversing with the young lad in the street, at the close of which the boy tipped his hat and went off. Moments later Holmes reappeared at the sitting-room door, his face grim.

"Bad news, Watson."

"What is it?"

He brandished the telegram.

"This is from Mrs. Hudson's sister in Cornwall."

"What does it say?"

Holmes read the message aloud. "'Martha in extreme danger: Come at once.'"

"Good Lord!"

Holmes stared grimly out the window.

"I am very sorry for my words yesterday, when I complained to you of ennui. I am reminded of an old Chinese curse: Be careful what you wish for, because you may get it." He turned to me, his face set. "I have gotten what I wished for, Watson."

Three

❧

Within minutes we were in a cab on our way to Waterloo Station. By the time we arrived there it was eleven-thirty. We saw on the departures board that there was a twelve o'clock train to Camelford, the nearest station to Tintagel, so Holmes went off to get our tickets. I stood under the departures board in the great central hall, which was bustling with people coming and going. Families bundled past us, dressed for a day's outing; young men and women stood in line waiting to buy tickets for their Sunday afternoon jaunt to the countryside.

As I stood watching the crowd, a curious little man with bushy muttonchop whiskers breezed past me and shoved a newspaper into my hands. Startled, I called after him, but he wove his way back into the crowd, quickly disappearing into the throng of people. I looked at the paper: it was today's *Telegraph,* though there was nothing remarkable about it that I could see.

"Look at this, Holmes," I said when my friend joined me, and did my best to describe the little man who had given it to me.

"Curiouser and curiouser," Holmes said, examining the paper closely. Then, glancing at the huge clock which overlooked the main hall of Waterloo Station, he said, "Come, Watson, we must hurry or we will miss our train."

Soon we were seated on a train bound for Cornwall, speeding through the English countryside with all the efficiency our modern rail system could muster. Fields and villages flew by: the grasslands on the outskirts of London were soon replaced by the rocky scrubble of Dorset and Devon. Mrs. Hudson's sister, Flora Campbell, lived near the town of Tintagel, noted not only for its excellent cream teas but also as the location of the ruins from which it takes its name–Tintagel–a medieval castle widely believed to be King Arthur's seat on the west coast of England. The castle, upon its rocky promontory overlooking the point where the Bristol Channel merges with the stormy waters of the Atlantic, attracted tourists from all over the world.

Holmes sat across from me, oblivious to the magnificent scenery, eagerly scanning the newspaper which the strange man had thrust at me. His keen eyes flickered about the pages restlessly. Suddenly his body went rigid.

"Here's a strange entry, Watson."

"What? What's strange?"

He handed me the paper and pointed to an entry in the classified ads. I read it out loud.

"'Mr. Fermat to Mr. Shomel: it's your move; your pawn is in deep water and speed is of the essence.' Now, what on earth does that mean? It sounds rather like a chess game of some kind."

Holmes' eyes narrowed.

"Yes, Watson," he said, "it *is* a chess game... but who is playing it, and why?"

He looked out the window at the heaths and meadows sweeping by, his face grim. "I am beginning to sense deeper waters than I ever would have imagined, Watson. I only hope that I am wrong."

When the train pulled into Camelford, located a few short miles from Tintagel, the only other people who disembarked from the train, besides ourselves, were a couple of hikers. They immediately shouldered their packs and took off across the windswept moors. Holmes and I stood on the platform for a few moments, and then went inside the tiny stationhouse. The sleepy stationmaster looked at us through one eye when Holmes asked about hiring transportation. He was a porridge-faced man, his skin white and lumpy as oatmeal, and he looked surprised when Holmes asked about cabs.

"Whar do yer need ta go?" he inquired in a heavy West Country accent.

"We have come to see Mrs. Flora Campbell."

The stationmaster nodded slowly, as though digesting the information.

"Jack Crompton's rig's just outside... Jack's around 'ere somewhere, I think. I'll just go see if I kin find 'im." With that, he shuffled out of the stationhouse, muttering to himself.

Holmes and I watched him go. I could sense that Holmes was losing what little patience he had; he was all twitches and tics, his long hands fidgeting at the buttons of his ulster.

"Come to think of it, why didn't Mrs. Campbell come to the station to greet us, I wonder?" I said finally.

"I was wondering the same thing, Watson," Holmes replied softly.

In a few moments our stationmaster returned with Jack Crompton, a hairy fellow whose salt-and-pepper locks and beard took up most of his face, leaving only enough space for his little raisin eyes and stubby red nose to poke through.

"Yer the ones wantin' a lift, are ye?" he said, scratching himself. At that moment I had the unpleasant thought that the rest of his body might be of the same excessively hirsute condition as his face.

Holmes stepped forward.

"Yes, please—and there's extra money in it if you can get us there quickly."

"Thar wantin' to see Flora Campbell," said the stationmaster with a wink.

"Aye, Flora Campbell, is it?" said Jack Crompton. "Well, I reckon my horse knows the way thar—I've delivered 'er milk these past five years with 'im. 'Ee's good horse, is my Bill," he said as we followed him out to the back of the stationhouse. A big white Clydesdale gelding stood dozing over a bucket of oats. He was harnessed to a surprisingly smart-looking trap, a little red two-wheeled gig. "Ee'd rather sleep than eat," said Jack Crompton, tossing the bucket into the back of the cart. "It's strange fer a horse, don't ye think?"

"Yes," I said politely, looking dubiously at the little rig. "Do you think there's room for all of us?"

"Aye, thar's room enough," said Jack Crompton as he hoisted himself onto the driver's seat and picked up the reins. "We've carried heavier loads than you two, 'aven't we, Bill?" he said, addressing the horse, who turned his gigantic head lazily toward us, giving us only the most cursory glance before returning to his nap. If ever a horse could have shrugged, this one would have done just that. Instead, he snorted and closed his eyes again. Holmes and I climbed aboard, squeezing in knee-to-knee behind Mr. Crompton.

"Aye, yer wouldn't believe 'ow much a load o' milk bottles weighs, I don't suppose," he said amiably, snapping the reins over the animal's broad back. To my surprise, the horse backed immediately, turned, and broke into a brisk trot.

"That's a well-trained horse you've got there, Mr. Crompton," I said as we clattered along the dirt road which seemed to be the only road to the train station.

"Aye, 'ee's a good horse, is my Bill." Crompton sighed happily. "Doesn't waste much energy—'ee's too smart for that. Aren't ye, Bill?" The big horse twitched his ears as if in reply.

We passed a few cottages sprinkled about the thin, rocky soil. They looked isolated and lonely out here on the moors, whitewashed walls bravely facing the sea, their little flower gardens desolate and windswept. Mrs. Campbell herself lived in a little white cottage a few miles from the station.

"Do yer want me to wait?" said Jack Crompton as we clambered down from our cramped seating position.

"Yes, if you don't mind," answered Holmes. "We may need you again. I'll see that you are well paid for your troubles," he called over his shoulder as we hurried up the path to the front door of the cottage, past a little windblown flower bed with some bedraggled-looking chrysanthemums.

When Mrs. Campbell greeted us at the front door of her house it was clear from the expression on her face that she was not expecting us. Like her sister, she was short and sturdy, with the ruddy complexion and fair hair of her Scottish ancestors.

"Why, Mr. Holmes, Dr. W-Watson," she stuttered after we introduced ourselves. "What are you doing here?" I was struck by how similar her voice was to her sister's; a little higher, perhaps, but there was the same faint but unmistakable Scottish cadence, the same Highland music in her speech.

"We got your telegram and came as quickly as we could," said Holmes.

"What telegram?" she asked, her broad face blank with surprise.

"The one saying your sister was in danger," I began, but Holmes cut me off.

"Never mind, Watson."

"But—" I protested.

"I'll explain *later*," Holmes said sharply. "Where is your sister?" he said to Mrs. Campbell.

"Why, she's out at Tintagel—"

"Did she say when she'd be back?"

Mrs. Campbell scratched her head. "Well, she's been gone an awfully long time, though I expect she stopped for lunch at the pub."

"We haven't a moment to lose!" cried Holmes. "Quickly, get your coat!"

Overriding Mrs. Campbell's confused protests, Holmes bundled her inside and returned a moment later with a thick red overcoat and long scarf.

"But I don't understand," she said as we hurried her back down the path to Jack Crompton's waiting carriage.

"I'll explain everything as we go," said Holmes. "But please believe me: We must hurry!"

"Tintagel Castle, if you please, Mr. Crompton," said Holmes, helping Mrs. Campbell climb up beside Jack Crompton. There was barely room for her broad frame on the narrow seat, and Crompton had to squeeze himself into the corner to accommodate her. As we all piled aboard, the big white gelding turned his head, looked at his new load with dismay, and sighed mightily.

"Don' worry, Bill, ye'll get extra oats for this, I promise," said Jack Crompton, and with a touch of the reins, we were off at a canter. The horse's big hooves dug into the damp soil, throwing clods of loose dirt out behind us.

"So your sister went to visit the castle?" said Holmes.

"Yes. She always likes to roam the rocks out there. Me, I don't see the point, but..." Mrs. Campbell wrung her hands. "What is it, Mr. Holmes—what's happened?"

"I hope nothing, Mrs. Campbell," said Holmes, "except that I believe speed is of the essence."

I was struck by his use of almost exactly the same phrase from the strange advertisement in the *Telegraph*.

"Who *did* send us that telegram, I wonder?" I said.

Holmes shook his head. "Whoever it was, they don't have our best interests in mind. They also know a lot about our movements. If I didn't know better, I would think... well, it's absurd, of course—and yet..." His voice trailed off and he subsided into a reverie.

For a while we all sat in silence as our gig bounced and rattled over the rocky ground, the horse's hooves beating a steady tattoo on the hard dirt of the road. Moisture pelted and stung our faces in tiny droplets, a combination of rain, mist, and sea spray. As we came over the crest of a hillock I could see the dark outline of Tintagel in the distance, gaunt and weatherbeaten from centuries of sea air.

When we arrived at the ruins, Jack Crompton turned his trap toward The Knights' Arms pub, a roadside establishment which evidently catered to thirsty tourists.

"There's a chance she might be warming her feet by the fireplace in the pub, Mr. Holmes," said Mrs. Campbell, her voice tremulous.

"Yes; we'd better check just to make certain," Holmes replied, vaulting out of his seat in one smooth motion. He disappeared into the pub but returned moments later, shaking his head.

"I'm afraid not—the barkeep hasn't seen anyone of her description all day," he said gently.

Mrs. Campbell nodded, her round face crinkled with worry.

"You'd best wait in there for us, Mrs. Campbell," said Holmes, but she shook her head.

"No, I want to come with you," she said firmly.

"Very well," said Holmes as I helped Mrs. Campbell down from her seat.

"I'll get Bill some water and wait for yer in there, if that's all right," Crompton called to us as we climbed up the rocky hill to the castle. The misty rain had stopped, but the sky was cloudy and the wind was still blowing in briskly from the sea. Our only company along the way was the hikers we had seen get off the train earlier. I guessed that they were Swiss tourists, complete with backpacks and lederhosen. They were coming back down the path as we ascended it. One of them had hair so blond it was almost white, with a natty little mustache to match. His cap was pulled down over his eyes, though, so that it was impossible to see much of his face.

Ahead of us we could see the ruins of Tintagel, dark and crumbling in the damp Cornwall air. When we arrived at the top Holmes looked around briefly, and then, without a word, threw himself face down upon the ground.

"Good heavens!" said our hostess, who was unused to my friend's eccentric behavior.

"Don't worry," I whispered to her. "He knows what he's doing."

After a few moments Holmes rose again and brushed the dirt from his hands.

"This way!" he said, and strode off in the direction of a crumbling stone archway.

After a few paces he stopped again, and, drawing a magnifying glass from his pocket, examined the soil. I stood shivering in the strong sea breeze, coat-tails whipping around my legs. We were on a ledge just outside the ruins, and I could smell the musty aroma of centuries of crumbling stones and dust. Below us the sea swirled and lapped fiercely at the jagged Cornish coastline.

"Observe, Watson," he said. "You see Mrs. Hudson's tracks going along the path here—"

"How do you know it's her?" said Mrs. Campbell in a querulous voice.

"Well, for one thing, the shoe print," said Holmes. "As you may know, your sister is very particular about her shoes, and always orders the same style from the same London cobbler. This damp ground is fortunately excellent for preserving prints—you see here the fine stitching? I also happen to know she favors her right side; she suffers from a touch of rheumatism in the cold weather, I believe—"

"Yes!" cried Mrs. Campbell. "It runs in the family; I myself often feel a touch of—"

"—and you see here how the right footstep is slightly fainter than the left? No, there is no question that this is our Mrs. Hudson. But this," Holmes continued, pointing to a larger man's print coming from the opposite direction, "this is very sinister. Here is also a London-made shoe; no one could mistake this gentleman for a local resident. You see how the prints meet here at the cliff's edge; there are signs of a scuffle, and then her tracks stop, but the other continues—"

"Good God, you're right!" I cried.

The implications of the footprints were all too clear: Holmes' poor landlady had met her death at the hands of whomever she had encountered at the top of this rocky promontory! I looked down at the swirling water below and suddenly felt once again the horror of that terrible day at Reichenbach Falls three years ago, the story mutely told by the two sets of footprints which vanished into the mist...

"Watson! Steady on!"

I recovered just in time to feel Holmes' strong grasp around my shoulders. I opened my eyes. I could not have blacked out for more than a second or two, and yet—

"Are you all right, Dr. Watson?" cried Mrs. Campbell, her round, worried face crinkled with concern.

"We almost lost you there for a moment, Watson," said Holmes, smiling grimly.

"If Mr. Holmes hadn't caught you, you would have fallen over the edge!" said Mrs. Campbell.

"I'm quite all right," I said, embarrassed. "Don't worry about me; it's Mrs. Hudson I'm concerned about. I'm afraid she—" I stopped myself, unable to say it.

"Ah! It may appear that way at first glance, but look!" said Holmes, pointing to the man's tracks which led away from the point of meeting, back in the direction in which he had come. "Do you see anything unusual about them?"

"Why, they're—deeper!" I cried. I inspected the footprints more closely. They did indeed sink more deeply into the soft black soil, the heels digging heavily into the dirt. "He—he must have been carrying her!"

"Can it be?" said Mrs. Campbell.

"It most certainly is," said Holmes. "We must follow these tracks—quickly! Mrs. Campbell," he said, turning to her, "do you know the schedule of high and low tides around these parts?"

"Well, yes, as a matter of fact, I make it my business—not that it's of much use to me nowadays. My father was a seagoing man, you see, and I got in the habit of always—"

"Yes, yes!" said Holmes impatiently. "Can you tell me when the next high tide will be today?"

"Why, yes; at six o'clock."

Holmes looked at his watch. "It is half past five! Quickly, Watson, we have very little time!"

I followed him as he hurried along the trail, nose to the ground. Mrs. Campbell trotted after us, her short little legs pumping rapidly to keep up with Holmes' long strides. Reaching a place where the path diverged and part of it sloped steeply down toward the water, Holmes turned to me.

"Just as I thought—he's headed for the caves!"

It was well known that the rocky coast of Cornwall was dotted with smugglers' caves which had been there for centuries. The caves weren't in use anymore, but children continued to explore them, and every so often one heard reports of a child being caught up in high tide and swept out to sea. I followed Holmes down the steep embankment. Mrs. Campbell stood at the top anxiously watching our progress, shawl blowing in the breeze, her short figure silhouetted against the increasingly stormy sky. I felt a few droplets of rain as Holmes and I made our way down the scraggly slope, our feet slipping and sliding on the loose pebbles which rolled down the hill and plunged into the foaming white water below.

"Steady on, Watson," said Holmes as my foot slipped and I slid a few feet down the muddy incline. I nodded and tried to pick my way more carefully, looking for footholds on the slippery bank. Finally we made it down to an overhanging ledge, with about ten feet of rocks between us and the rushing water below. Holmes stepped carefully along the ledge, his eyes searching the rocks for any sign of an indentation.

"There—look, Watson, there it is!" he cried suddenly, pointing to a gap in the rocks where water was pouring in. It did indeed appear to be a cave set in the side of the cliff; the water which flowed in did not seem to be coming back out. "The tide, Watson; it's rushing in—we must hurry!" he said. I followed Holmes as he scrambled down the ragged, jutting rocks, cutting my hands on their jagged edges as I went.

We reached the entrance of the cave and looked inside. It was very black, and my heart sank when I saw that the water had already begun to rise inside so that it was at least a foot deep. Holmes did not hesitate, though, and plunged right into the freezing water. I took a deep breath and followed him.

The water on England's west coast, fed by northern oceanic currents, never reaches anything near swimming temperature, and the shock of that water took my breath away. It was icy and biting, making my legs feel numb within seconds of contact. Holmes strode on ahead, though, and I trudged after him, puffing in an attempt to regain my wind.

Within moments we heard what we had come for. From the center of the horrible damp darkness came a sound which was more welcome to my ears than any I could imagine: Through the pounding of the surf upon the rocks, we heard the faint but unmistakable sound of Mrs. Hudson's voice calling to us.

"Mrs. Hudson!" bellowed Holmes.

"Here—over here!" came her voice from the depths of rock and water. As my eyes became accustomed to the darkness I could just make out the figure of a woman huddled against a rock. Within seconds Holmes and I had splashed our way over to her and Holmes held her in his arms.

"Oh, Mr. Holmes, I thought I was—oh, thank God, thank God—oh, Dr. Watson!" she babbled, quite hysterical. I can't say that I blamed her. When I thought of the fate from which we had narrowly saved her, I think I would have been hysterical myself.

Holmes carried her back across the torrent of water. The tide was truly pouring in in earnest now, and, in the onslaught of foaming seawater, he lost his footing and stumbled.

"Are you all right, Holmes?" I called over the din of rushing water.

"Yes, Watson—we must get out as quickly as possible!" he called back, and we pressed on. I couldn't feel my legs at all now. The water had risen past my knees, and the numbness was creeping up my body. Still, we sloshed our way through the torrent of incoming tide, and finally reached the safety of the rock ledge. I climbed upon the slippery shelf and Holmes handed Mrs. Hudson up to me. Then, with one final burst of energy, Holmes pulled himself up onto the rock, just as a spray of water hit and threatened to suck us all back into the deluge which we had so narrowly escaped.

It was only then that I noticed Mrs. Hudson was bound hand and foot. Even if she had the heart to try to escape through that terrifying black cave, she would have been unable to do so. I quickly loosened her bonds, but she was still beside herself with emotion.

"Oh, Dr. Watson!" she cried, and fell weeping upon my shoulder. I looked at Holmes: he was evidently moved. Though in control as always, I could see by his strained face the emotional and physical toll this near tragedy had taken on him.

"Your sister is waiting for us at the top," said Holmes after a moment. "I think we shouldn't keep her in suspense any longer than necessary."

The three of us straggled up the hill. It had begun to rain in earnest now, and we were a sorry sight by the time we reached Flora Campbell. When she saw her sister, she could not contain herself, but came half running, half sliding down the hill to meet us.

"Oh, Martha, thank God you're alive! Oh, thank God!" she cried over and over, as the two sisters fell into each other's arms.

We were a strange sight staggering through the door of The Knights' Arms pub, but the landlord looked at us with a face as blank and unreadable as a stone. Jack Crompton sat at a table in the corner, a pint of bitter in front of him. He shook his head when he saw us.

"'T is a strange day for roamin' these rocks," he said, downing the last of his beer. "Come on, then, let's get you back home."

Bill the Clydesdale stood out the back of the pub, a stolid expression on his big blunt face. The rain pelted his back as steam rose from his thick coat, now more gray than white, sprinkled with splotches of mud and dirt. The smoky smell of damp horsehair hung in the air.

"Oh, poor Bill," said Flora Campbell as we climbed aboard the now sodden rig.

"Oh, don't worry," said Jack Crompton. "Horses don' mind standin' in the rain—do ye, Bill?"

Bill looked at his master and sighed heavily.

"'Ee's a good boy, is my Bill," said Jack Crompton cheerfully, taking up the reins.

It was a bedraggled crew that arrived at Flora Campbell's cottage a short while later, wet and miserable and chilled to the bone. Jack Crompton refused Mrs. Campbell's offer of hospitality. Though she importuned him to come inside and get warm, he shook his head.

"Thank yer kindly, but I'd best get Bill back to 'is barn an' a nice bucket o' fresh oats," he said, tipping his hat. Holmes paid him handsomely for his trouble, and Crompton whistled merrily as he returned to the long-suffering Bill, who stood sullenly at the bottom of Mrs. Campbell's garden, thoroughly drenched.

It wasn't long before we were all huddled around a roaring fire, cups of tea held between our stiffened fingers, blankets around our shoulders. The room was suffused with the sweet smell of burning sod. (There aren't many trees in Cornwall, and sod is often the fuel of choice for heating fires.) I told the sisters about the mysterious telegram, as well as the strange newspaper advertisement. By that time poor Mrs. Hudson had calmed down considerably, and Holmes wasted no time in pumping her for information about her abduction.

"I was wandering along the cliffs, you know, not thinking about much of anything, when I saw a man coming toward me from the other direction. He stopped and asked me politely if I had the time. I told him that I didn't and turned to go but that's when he grabbed me..." She stopped, quite overcome by emotion. Holmes averted his eyes, always embarrassed by any display of feelings, but Mrs. Campbell put her arms around her sister.

"Don't you worry, dearie," she said. "You just have a good cry, there's a good girl."

But Mrs. Hudson recovered herself and continued.

"I struggled, of course, and even cried out, but there was no one to hear me. The pub is too far away, way down at the bottom of the hill by the road—"

"There were no tourists, no other hikers?" said Holmes.

"You saw what kind of a day it was, Mr. Holmes," Mrs. Hudson said almost apologetically. "I'm afraid I was the only one foolish enough to walk about on a day like today."

"We actually saw some others, some Swiss hikers," I said.

Holmes looked at me. "Yes, so we did," he said. "Did you happen to get a good look at them, Watson?"

"Well, not a very long look, but—"

"Did you notice anything peculiar about them?"

I tried to think. "Oh, I did notice that the one man had very light hair—not white exactly, but that's why it struck me. It was unusual, you know?"

"Yes," said Holmes, "yes, I know."

"I couldn't make out his face, though, because his cap was pulled so low over his eyes, and he was looking at the ground when he passed us."

"Yes," said Holmes. "I wonder…" His keen eyes narrowed. The three of us sat quietly sipping our tea, afraid to say anything for fear of spoiling his concentration. After a minute he broke out of his reverie and addressed Mrs. Hudson once again.

"This man who abducted you—can you describe him? Had you ever seen him before?"

Mrs. Hudson looked into the fire and bit her lip.

"He was big, very big—I would say well over six feet, and he was very strong. I'm not exactly a small woman," she said, referring to her comfortable girth, "and yet he picked me up as though I were a child. His hands..." She stopped and shuddered. Mrs. Campbell patted her sister's hand sympathetically. "His hands were huge—big and rough, very rough, as a workman's hands might be after years of manual labor."

"Excellent!" cried Holmes, and we all looked at him. He was not insensitive to Mrs. Hudson's pain, and yet, for him, the facts now superseded any other factors in the case. "What about his face?" he said. "Did you get a look at his face?"

"What I remember is that his eyes were red, small and red like a pig's eyes. His skin was ruddy, as though he had spent a lot of time outdoors... all his features were blunt and indistinct, kind of like a face pressed up against a windowpane, you know?"

Holmes leaned back in his chair. "Mrs. Hudson, you have acquitted yourself well! In spite of the terror which you experienced during this horrible event, you managed to do a credible job noticing and remembering important details. I congratulate you!"

Mrs. Hudson blushed and smiled. In spite of her tremulous state, Holmes' words were high praise indeed, and they did as much to warm her as any fire.

"One last thing. Can you tell me anything about his voice?"

"It was like a growl. Very low and rumbling, like thunder you hear from way off."

"Well done, Mrs. Hudson, well done indeed."

"What I don't understand is how you knew poor Martha was in trouble," said Mrs. Campbell.

Holmes shrugged. "I couldn't afford to take a chance. The telegram combined with the newspaper advertisement added up to a sinister conclusion, to say the least."

"Who would do a thing like this?" asked Mrs. Campbell.

"I don't know," said Holmes, "although I have my suspicions."

"Mr. Holmes has ever so many criminals who wish to get even with him," Mrs. Hudson said to her sister with an air of pride. Even after her narrow escape, she evidently felt honored to be a part of Holmes' work, a feeling I knew well myself. However, I had to admire her pluck. I suspect that many people who had just been through what she had might have been considerably more flustered. I also knew, though, that her relative peace of mind was due to something that all of us who knew Holmes felt: His very presence encouraged a feeling of security, so that when one was around him one had the impression that no matter what happened Holmes would know what to do. It was a way he had about him, this ability to inspire confidence in others. In fact, I had on occasion remarked that if he had chosen a military career he would have been an outstanding general.

"What I don't understand is why they didn't just kill me outright," said Mrs. Hudson, stirring her tea.

"Yes, that is most certainly important," said Holmes. "One obvious reason is that they did not wish to incur my undying wrath."

Mrs. Hudson blushed at this remark with its implied compliment.

"At any rate," Holmes said, "you are no longer in danger. Now, I think," he continued, rising from his chair by the fire, "Watson and I will leave you in the care of your sister and return to London."

"Won't you consider staying a while, Mr. Holmes?" said Mrs. Campbell anxiously. "I mean, aren't you just a little afraid that whoever did this will—well, will try again?"

"If my theory is correct, you are both quite safe now," said Holmes, "and we should get back to London as soon as possible. But if it will make you feel better, I suppose Watson and I could spend the night—that is, if there's room."

"Oh, there's plenty of room," said Mrs. Campbell. "This cottage was built for a family, and now there's just me here. There's a storm on its way, and I'd be very glad if you would consent to spend the night."

I looked outside: A storm was indeed gathering, the wind tossing the trees back and forth like a dog worrying a rag, their trunks bending and swaying in the gale. Travel on such a night would be difficult if not downright impossible.

"What do you say, Watson—can you stay the night?" said Holmes, much to my relief. I had no wish to venture out in the approaching storm.

"Yes, I believe I can," I said with a deliberate casualness. I didn't want Holmes to know that I was loathe to leave the warmth of Mrs. Campbell's hearth for the fury which awaited us outside.

"Very well, Mrs. Campbell, thank you for your hospitality," said Holmes.

"Good!" said our hostess, clapping her hands together like an excited child. "I hope you have no aversion to steak and kidney pie for dinner?"

"None whatsoever," Holmes replied. "In fact, I believe it is one of Dr. Watson's favorites."

"It most certainly is," interjected Mrs. Hudson, who was rapidly regaining her old form. "He likes it with a bit of cress on the side. Do you have any fresh watercress, Flora?"

"I believe I do," said Mrs. Campbell. "It grows out by the stream, and I picked some just yesterday."

"I'll make the pudding," said Mrs. Hudson. "I'll just need a few fresh eggs, some vanilla, and a few other things I'm sure you have."

The two sisters headed for the kitchen, chatting about the upcoming meal, leaving Holmes and myself alone before the glowing embers of the fire.

"The man who abducted Mrs. Hudson—did he sound familiar?" I asked after a few moments.

"Oh, he did indeed, though I haven't seen him for some years; I thought he was still in prison. A nasty character—George Simpson by name, an East End sewer rat who used to do the dirtiest sorts of jobs for Professor Moriarty. I sent him to Newgate Prison some years ago and haven't heard of him since." Holmes got up and stirred the dying embers back to life. "It certainly sounds like him, though I wonder how he managed to get out of Newgate..."

After that Holmes lapsed into silence, fingertips pressed together, sitting deep in his chair, his gray eyes staring into the fire, until we were called for dinner.

Mrs. Campbell's steak and kidney pie was as good as advertised, and after our exertions of the day, I ate heartily, gulping down large quantities of gingery Cornish ale. Holmes, however, didn't eat very much at all. We were all exhausted, and retired to bed soon after dinner. Lying between the clean starched sheets of our attic bedroom, feeling drowsy from the beer, I should have fallen asleep immediately. However, sleep did not come. I listened to the fury of the wind outside, howling and wailing, pressing up eagerly against the eaves. We were safe inside the thick walls of the cottage, though, that had been built to withstand such gales. I settled deeper into the goose-down quilt comforter, and dozed off for a while. I awoke suddenly and sat bolt upright in bed. The room was still. No noise had awakened me, but I noticed that Holmes was not in his bed. My eyes could just make out his tall, spare form, seated by the window. He sat perfectly still, staring out into the night, his sharp profile silhouetted by the occasional flash of lightning far in the distance. The storm was moving off.

"Holmes?"

"Yes, Watson?"

"Who... who do you think is behind all of this?"

There was a silence, and then he spoke, his voice far away.

"A ghost, Watson—a ghost."

Four

&

We rose early the next morning, and Holmes reluctantly accepted an offer of breakfast. He did it on my behalf, I think. Whatever the reason, I was glad enough to fortify myself with Mrs. Campbell's excellent Scotch porridge and hot tea before we left for the train station.

"Are you sure we'll be all right?" said Mrs. Campbell as we waited for the train to London.

"Yes, quite sure," said Holmes. "Stay in touch by telegram if you should see anything unusual, but I shouldn't worry if I were you."

As the train pulled into the station, a thick cloud of black smoke pouring from its smokestack, Mrs. Campbell impetuously hugged us both. I found the gesture touching, but I could tell it made Holmes uncomfortable. Mrs. Hudson and I exchanged a wry glance at the behavior of her sister. Still, Holmes bade both sisters a warm farewell, and the last thing I saw was the two of them, arm in arm, waving to us as the train pulled away.

Holmes settled into our compartment with a copy of the *Telegraph,* which he had purchased at the station. He seemed to be looking for something, and he evidently found it, because he gave an exclamation and held the paper out to me.

"See, Watson—another message like the one yesterday: here."

I took the paper and read the entry in the classifieds:

"'Mr. Fermat to Mr. Shomel: you have thwarted my knight but my pawn captures your pawn. The sword has been pulled from the stone, but at what cost?'"

I handed the paper back to Holmes.

"What does it mean, I wonder?"

"Oh, the meaning is clear enough," he said grimly. "The sword in the stone is a reference to King Arthur. As for the recipient, the message is evidently intended for me."

"So the message is for *you*?"

"Watson, surely the crude anagram of 'Shomel' did not escape you," Holmes said impatiently. "That the message is for me I have no doubt. It is who is sending it that has me worried."

"Who do you think it is?"

"We are being watched, Watson. Our every move is being followed, and I cannot but think that we ourselves are being used as pawns in a much bigger game."

"Watched? Who is watching us?"

"Watson, you yourself noticed the Swiss 'tourists' yesterday, but you failed to notice the most telling thing about them."

"What was that?"

"Their shoes."

"Their shoes?"

"Yes. I remarked it at once: Their shoes were brand new."

"Well, I don't see how that—"

"Consider, Watson. Any experienced hiker knows that you do not go on a lengthy holiday with a new pair of shoes. You buy your shoes well ahead of time and wear them in properly, otherwise you end up with blisters. So when I asked myself what self-respecting hikers would go out so foolishly wearing brand-new shoes, I came to the conclusion that they were not hikers at all: in short, that they were impostors."

"Impostors!"

"Yes, Watson: they were sent there to spy on us."

"But—why?"

"Why indeed?" Holmes held up the newspaper. "You see our actions have been carefully noted here. If they had wanted to kill Mrs. Hudson, it would have been easy enough, but instead she was captured and we were lured away to save her—which it was possible to do if we read all the signs exactly right."

I looked at the newspaper again.

"So you are Mr. Shomel—I see that now clearly enough. But who is Mr. Fermat?"

"That is what worries me, Watson. It is impossible, and yet…" He stared out the window at the rolling countryside, the tidy hedgerows and farm fields giving way to villages. "I wonder, do ghosts rise from the dead?"

When we returned to Baker Street, a small, shabby boy was leaning up against the building which housed 221B. I recognized him as Tuthill, Holmes' most trusted member of the Baker Street Irregulars.

"Mr. Holmes!" he said when he saw us. "I've been waiting for you ever so long. I've kept an eye on the place for you just as you asked."

"I appreciated that, Master Tuthill," Holmes said in a kindly voice. "Why don't you come upstairs and have something to refresh yourself, and then you can tell us what you've seen."

"'Ta very much," Master Tuthill said gratefully, bounding up the stairs after us.

After he had put away the better part of the joint of cold beef, Tuthill sat back in his chair and gazed at us with warm eyes. It was evident from the way he tucked into the meat that he could do with a few more meals like that.

"So, what do you have to tell us?" Holmes said, lighting his pipe.

Tuthill pushed away the lank strands of dirty blond hair which hung over his eyes and wiped some of the smudges from his cheeks with a dirty sleeve. "I don't know as how it's important or not, but you told me to always report to you if I sees anything strange like."

"Yes, yes, quite right, Tuthill," said Holmes. "What is it that you saw?"

"Well, you know how you told me to keep an eye on that poor crippled fellow, Mr. Wiggins?"

"Yes?"

"Well, Billy Kimball's been watchin' him regular like, only yesterday he gets no answer when he knocks."

"And–?"

"That's all. I just thought I should tell you."

"Did Billy see anyone suspicious lurking around Mr. Wiggins' place?"

"No, sir. I asked 'im that myself, and 'e says 'e didn't see nobody."

"Thank you, Master Tuthill; you have done well to report this to me."

"I–I hope there's nothing the matter, sir. Mr. Wiggins, 'e's a nice man–all the fellows think so, sir."

"Don't worry; I shall look into the matter myself."

"Yes, sir." Tuthill stood and straightened his ragged clothes. Though he was old enough to wear long pants, his well-worn breeches barely covered his thin knees. "Thank you for the beef, sir."

"You're quite welcome, Tuthill. Why don't you take some with you when you go?"

"Oh, I couldn't, sir…"

"Go ahead. We won't eat it all."

Tuthill managed to stuff an amazing amount of roast beef into his pockets, along with a couple of thick slices of bread, and then he left. Holmes closed the door after him with a sigh.

"There are thousands of street urchins like him out there, Watson. The problem grows larger every day, and yet society doesn't seem to think it important enough to do anything about it. I'll tell you one thing: The Tuthills of this world are headed for a life of crime unless someone steps in between them and the hard life they've been forced to live."

"Someone like you?" I said with a smile. I had always wondered if the Irregulars were Holmes' own secret charity case, one he could indulge in without exposing his sentiments, on the pretext that the ragged boys and girls he sponsored helped him solve his cases. That they occasionally did help him, I had no doubt. But the coins he regularly distributed among them were far out of proportion to the services he required of them. Holmes was already putting on his coat.

"Come, Watson," he said. "I am disturbed by what Tuthill has told us."

I quickly fetched my own coat and hat.

"You don't think…?"

"I don't know, but I intend to find out."

There was no sign of the storm which had blown so bitterly in Cornwall. In fact, London was being visited by a rare period of bright sunshine. It was not hard to find a cab in such weather, and within minutes we were on our way once again to Mr. Wiggins' extraordinary establishment under the shadow of St. Paul's Church.

The same narrow street did not look so threatening in broad daylight, and, as we stood in front of Wiggins' door, I looked about me and saw that some of the other establishments on the street were quite respectable: Facing onto the alley were the back entrances of a cobbler's shop, a saddler, and a silversmith. We stepped over a small pile of rotting vegetables and knocked on the door. There was no answer to our knocks, however, and when Holmes pushed lightly on the door it opened. Holmes looked at me, his face grim.

"Be careful, Watson," he said. "I don't know what we'll find inside."

Upon entering the shop I felt at once that something was horribly wrong. We were greeted by a piteous, high-pitched keening, much like the wailing of a small child. The sound came from Bandu the parrot, who was at his usual place behind the counter. However, as soon as we closed the door behind us, the noise abruptly ceased. The silence was as startling as the wailing had been. The perfume bottles sat upon their shelves, their rich colors reflecting in the gas light, and Bandu sat upon his perch, gazing at us with his bright orange eyes, but there was no sign of Wiggins.

Holmes turned to me, his face rigid.

"There has been foul play here, Watson, foul play indeed."

I followed Holmes through an ocher brocade curtain that separated the front room from a narrow hallway which led to the rear of the building: Wiggins' laboratory. As we walked down the hallway I inhaled the smell of a hundred different scents, some sharp and clear as a mountain stream, some musky, others flowery and sweet. I felt quite dizzy by the time we entered the room.

When we entered the laboratory, we found the pitiful sight which we so dreaded. Wiggins was seated at his laboratory desk, clad in a white lab coat, his body slumped over in the chair. It was immediately clear to me that he was dead.

Holmes stood for several moments, still as a statue, then he turned to me. His normally impassive face was suffused with such fury that I took a step backwards, startled in spite of myself.

"By God, Watson, whoever did this to Wiggins will pay! I swear to you I will avenge his death with my own hands!" he hissed through clenched teeth.

I said nothing, afraid to interrupt Holmes in this mood. I looked around the room: It was a well-stocked laboratory, with shining modern equipment set out upon two large tables. Another set of specially constructed shelves held small vials of fragrance samples as well as spare equipment: beakers, test tubes, pipettes, and Petri dishes. Wiggins had been justifiably proud of his laboratory, and I remembered sadly his promise to show it to us upon our next visit. I turned to Holmes, who was examining Wiggins' body.

"What do you make of this, Watson?" he said.

I examined Wiggins' body. There were no visible wounds, but redness around the neck area and the purplish cast to his face indicated strangulation. I told Holmes this, and he nodded grimly.

"Damn that storm! We never should have stayed in Cornwall last night," he said bitterly. "I was right when I suspected they wanted me out of London."

"Yes, but even if you were in London, I doubt that you would have prevented this," I said gently.

"Perhaps not, but now the trail is cold."

"It wouldn't have been difficult to kill him, you know. The condition he suffers from frequently makes it difficult for the sufferer to breathe normally anyway…" I looked at his poor, pathetic form. If ever a man had not deserved what fate had dealt him, it was Wiggins. "But who would want Wiggins dead?" I wondered out loud.

"That is precisely what I intend to find out," Holmes replied, his face set, jaw clenched.

"We shall have to inform the police, you know," I said.

"Yes, yes, but first we must see what clues we can find before they come along and spoil everything," Holmes replied impatiently, inspecting the floor around Wiggins' desk. "Here's a little something," he said, picking it up and examining it under the lamp.

"What is it?"

"A hair, Watson."

"Oh?"

"Yes, but not one of Wiggins' hairs; perhaps it is the hair of the murderer. In any case, it is very light–almost white–and very coarse."

I tried to imagine an old, white-haired man killing the unfortunate Wiggins, but it didn't seem likely.

"Very well," said Holmes after inspecting the crime scene thoroughly. "I shall leave the rest for Scotland Yard. Come, Watson, let us see if they have left clues for us anywhere else."

I followed Holmes back through the cramped hallway into the front room of the shop. Bandu appeared very excited to see us, bouncing up and down on his perch.

"B-b-be quiet!" he said loudly. "B-b-be quiet, y-y-you idiot!"

Holmes stopped where he was and looked at the parrot.

"Did you hear that, Watson?" he said.

"Yes, he said 'Be quiet, you–' "

"I *know* what he said!" Holmes hissed impatiently. "It's *how he said it* that matters!"

As if to oblige, the parrot repeated his comment.

"B-b-be quiet, y-y-you idiot!"

"That's it–do you see, Watson?" said Holmes.

"You mean, he's stuttering?" I said.

"Yes!" said Holmes. "Wiggins never stuttered."

"Maybe one of his clients–"

"Do you remember what Wiggins said about this parrot? That he liked to pick up new sayings, and that he was always changing his latest phrases?"

"Yes, I remember."

"Don't you *see*, Watson: there were two men here, not one, and the parrot is repeating what one of the men said to the other!"

"Good God—you're right, Holmes!"

He removed the hair from his pocket and looked at it under the light. His face darkened and he put the hair back in his pocket.

"I think it's time to pay a visit to Freddie Stockton."

Of all the nasty fellows Holmes and I had dealt with over the years, there were few nastier than Freddie Stockton. I had first come across him during The Strange Case of the Tongue-Tied Tenor, during his employment by Professor Moriarty before the fall at Reichenbach cut short his illustrious criminal career. After Moriarty's death, Stockton worked for Colonel Moran for a while, and then, after that gentleman was jailed through Holmes' efforts, Stockton turned to various pursuits: blackmail, theft, and the occasional beating. Holmes had once told me that even among London criminal society it was said of Freddie Stockton that he would strangle his own grandmother for the price of a pint. Physically, Stockton was distinguished by two striking characteristics: his profuse whitish blond hair and a pronounced stutter.

Now Holmes and I were in search of this princely character. After procuring a hansom cab Holmes gave the driver instructions to take us to the East End, where the mix of poverty and predators created a dangerous and squalid environment.

"Do you remember the Swiss tourists we saw in Cornwall, Watson?" Holmes said, leaning against the window of our cab as it swayed back and forth upon the cobblestones.

"Yes," I answered. "One of them had whitish blond hair, just like Stockton. Do you think it's possible that he was one of the tourists?"

"I think it not only possible but likely," said Holmes grimly. "Unfortunately I barely glanced at him—as you can imagine, my mind was on other things. And, as you noticed, his cap was hiding most of his face. He must have come straight back to London after we saw him—he may even have thought we recognized him."

Our cab stopped in front of a low, unsavory tavern called The Drowned Rat. The sign hanging above the entrance had a picture of a waterlogged rodent, evidently deceased. Holmes paid the driver and we alighted.

"Watch yourself among these men, Watson," Holmes said before we went in. "They would just as soon pull a knife on you as look at you."

I nodded, wishing I had brought along my service revolver. I took a deep breath and followed Holmes into the tavern.

If any of the clientele in this charming establishment actually had no criminal record, it wasn't immediately obvious. One would be hard pressed to find a more hardened, depraved, or menacing crew than the one gathered at The Drowned Rat. Holmes and I were so clearly an anomaly among this crowd—just by virtue of the way we were dressed, if nothing else—that I feared for our safety. Several rough-looking fellows stared at us when we entered, but Holmes strode straight ahead with his usual confidence and they left us alone. Evidently they felt we weren't worth bothering about. We made our way through the cloud of tobacco smoke to the bar, where the huge and unkempt bartender ignored us for as long as he possibly could before finally asking us what we wanted. Holmes gazed at him calmly.

"Freddie Stockton," he said evenly.

The bartender blinked, and then he laughed, showing his large, discolored teeth.

"Now what would fine gentl'men like you be wantin' with the likes o' Freddie?"

Holmes did not smile; not a muscle moved on his taut face. The bartender fidgeted with his filthy rag, and then he frowned.

"Freddie's not 'ere right now."

"Then find us someone who can tell us where he is."

The bartender looked as if he were about to say something, and then he shrugged.

"Well, I s'pose Wickham would know."

"And where can I find him?"

"'E's in t' back room."

Without a word Holmes turned and walked in the direction the bartender had indicated, through a corridor which led to a dark and foul-smelling back room. A dozen or so men were seated on benches around a pit in which a small white terrier was shaking a rat that it held between its teeth. The pit was littered with the corpses of rats who had already met their fate in the fangs of this ferocious beast. The men were laughing and egging on the terrier with cries of, "Go, Billy!" and "Come on, finish him off!"

The stench in the room was vile, a disgusting combination of stale smoke, sweat, sawdust, and death. A couple of the men looked up at us as we entered.

"Is Wickham here?" Holmes said loudly.

Several of the men snickered. A fat, hairy-armed man shoved a tattooed elbow into the side of the fellow sitting next to him.

"Oi, Wickham, didn't you 'ear the gentl'man—yer *wanted*!"

His companion was a tall, thin, bespectacled man—singular among this crowd—with a look of corrupted respectability. He peered nervously at Holmes and myself.

"Are you Wickham?" said Holmes sternly.

"What if I am?" he replied with an attempt at a sneer that came off as a sulk.

Holmes walked up to Wickham and grasped him by the collar, practically lifting him up off his seat.

"Then I hope for your sake you can tell me what I need to know," he said, pulling the man's face close to his.

Wickham's face reddened, though I could not tell if it was from fright or from the fact that Holmes was cutting off his air supply. In any event, he managed to choke out a reply.

"All right; all right, guv'ner—what do you want to know?"

Holmes released his grasp on Wickham.

"Just this: Where is Freddie Stockton?"

Wickham rubbed his throat and looked around for help, but his comrades were enjoying the spectacle of his interrogation more than the efforts of the energetic Billy, who had just sent two more rats off to meet their maker.

"Well, I–I suppose you might find 'im at Penny Annie's about now," Wickham said, his voice shaking. "It's in Lambeth—just ask anyone."

Holmes stared at the man as if assessing the veracity of his statement. Then, evidently satisfied, he turned around and, without a word, left the room. I followed after, hearing as I went the taunting voices of Wickham's comrades: "Oo, what 'a ya done now, Wickham, my boy?" and "Good thing you told 'im or 'eed 'a turned you into terrier meat!" followed by shrill, raucous laughter.

Holmes left the pub without so much as a glance at the bartender or any of the rough lot who looked us over as we made our way out. Holmes seemed utterly unconcerned by the sullen faces which squinted up at us from the various tables, although I for one was glad to get out of there. It is a facet of my friend's character that when he is focused on a task he cares little for his own personal safety. However, I am more easily intimidated, and I breathed a sigh of relief when we stood once more in the cold night air of the London street. I took a deep breath; even the London atmosphere was an improvement upon the fetid air we had just left.

I wanted to say something to Holmes, but, seeing his determined face in the lamplight, I couldn't think of what to say. We hailed a cab and soon we were among the winding streets of Lambeth. The cab pulled up alongside a row of respectable-looking shops, and I could see light coming from the upper stories of the buildings. As we climbed out of the cab, the sound of shouting and laughter greeted our ears, almost drowning out the sound of music coming from the upper floors of the buildings. People were coming and going in and out of the buildings, in groups or in pairs. Most were shabbily dressed, their faces flushed with drink, arms flung around each other in a casual camaraderie made easy by cheap gin. Holmes stopped one of the more respectable-looking couples.

"Can you tell me which of these establishments is Penny Annie's?"

The woman, who hung somewhat crookedly on her companion's arm, straightened up and regarded Holmes with a smile. Her lipstick was smeared, and her half-closed eyes indicated her inebriated state. A soiled yellow silk shawl hung rakishly over one shoulder.

"Why do you want to go in there, luv?" she said.

"Hey, sod that," said her companion, a short, muscular man who was dressed in a striped sailor's shirt.

"Oh, go to, Eddie, I'm just 'aving fun," she said, turning to Holmes. "It's the one on the end—there." She pointed to a brightly lit establishment with the tinny sound of a concertina coming from its windows.

"Thank you," said Holmes.

"Any time," she said as her companion pulled her away. I could hear them arguing as Holmes and I made our way to our destination.

"You're my girl, Mary. Why do you make me suffer so?"

"Oh, Eddie, don't fuss at me; it's only in fun."

Penny Annie's was one of the many "penny gaffs" which were to be found all over the city: places where disreputable performers sang and danced for a variety of customers. After the show the "performers" were often available for a more private engagement.

As Holmes and I ascended a staircase littered with walnut shells and orange peels, we could hear the laughter and shouting above us mixing with the stalwart concertina, which droned on bravely through the din. I could just barely hear a penny whistle weaving in and out of the melody. The "theatre" was comprised of a converted flat: a rough stage had been constructed at one end of the long room, and benches had been set along the floor. A motley crowd sat upon these seats—sailors and dock workers mixed with some who appeared to be office employees on a night out. Dustmen rubbed shoulders with prosperous-looking merchants; and a few of the customers wore the distinctive red silk neckerchiefs which labeled them as costermongers, or street vendors.

One customer stood out, though, even if you weren't looking for him. Burly, with muscular shoulders and a snarl for a smile, he was like many of the other men we had seen tonight, except that he was distinguished by his striking complexion. His hair was so blond that it was almost white, and his skin was so pale that it shone like a beacon from among the ruddy, sunburned lot who surrounded him. I recognized him immediately as the second Swiss tourist we had seen upon the moor, though he was now without his little mustache.

"Stay here, Watson!" Holmes hissed, and began to make his way through the crowd. Stockton was seated on one of the benches in the back, and could not see Holmes approach. I stood at my post by the door and looked at the stage. A suggestively dressed woman well past forty years old was dancing to the tunes which the concertina player continued to grind out; she jiggled and bobbed, flipped her skirts and displayed whatever she could to the grinning customers in the front row, who whistled and grabbed at her. She was too quick for them, though, and they always ended up with a fistful of air for their efforts. They didn't seem to mind, and howled with laughter, cheering her on.

The woman's thick curly hair had been dyed an improbable shade of red, her make-up was running in rivulets down her sweaty cheeks—so that one had the impression she was crying rainbow-colored tears—and yet there was something both game and touching about her. She was giving her customers their money's worth, and I had to admire her dogged energy and determination. The concertina player sat, cigarette hanging from his lips, reeling off tune after tune, gazing implacably above the heads of his listeners.

Holmes had reached his destination, and I looked up just in time to see him place a hand on Freddie Stockton's collar. Stockton hadn't seen him coming, and, when he saw Holmes, real terror passed over his unpleasant face. Holmes half dragged him through the crowd over to where I was standing.

"Let's go, Watson," he said, and we left the theatre.

Once outside, Holmes dragged Stockton around to the side of the building and held him up against the wall.

"All right, Stockton, let's hear it, and it had better be convincing," said Holmes.

"I d-d-don't know what you're t-t-talking about," Stockton said sullenly.

"Oh yes you do, and it will go better for you if you talk sooner rather than later." He held Stockton about six inches off the ground. "Now, you have exactly one minute to tell me why you killed Jeremiah Wiggins."

Holmes was not a violent man, but I don't like to think what he would have done to Stockton if the man had not confessed.

"It w-w-wasn't supposed to happen like that; I d-d-didn't *do* anything to him," Stockton muttered.

"Didn't *do* anything to him?" Holmes said, his voice hoarse with rage. "He's dead, and you didn't *do* anything to him?"

"Well, not m-m-much, anyway. I just… t-t-tried to s-s-scare him a little… and all of a s-s-sudden 'e was d-d-d-dead."

Holmes tightened his grip on Stockton's throat, and, not wanting my friend to answer to murder charges himself, I put my hand on his shoulder.

"Holmes," I said softly.

"What *is* it, Watson?" he answered irritably.

"His condition—the disease—it would have made strangling him by accident quite easy. As I mentioned before, one of the side effects of his condition is difficulty—"

"All right!" Holmes said angrily, and loosened his grasp on Stockton. "Someone else was there with you—who was it?"

"Wickham… the idiot," Stockton added under his breath, referring to the prim, bespectacled young man we had just seen at The Drowned Rat.

"What were you there for then, if not to kill him?"

Stockton hesitated, and then, seeing Holmes meant business, muttered, "W-w-we was supposed to g-g-get information—"

"Information? About what?"

"About why you was there. B-b-but 'e wouldn't t-t-talk, and so's I 'ad to convince 'im, an' that's when…" Stockton stopped and looked at Holmes almost contritely. "I didn't m-m-mean to k-k-kill 'im."

"I believe you," said Holmes, "but why was it so important to know why we were there?"

Stockton looked around desperately, and then he closed his eyes as though expecting a blow.

"G-g-go ahead, k-k-kill me," he said. "If I t-t-tell you, '*e'll* kill me anyway."

"Who? Who will kill you?"

"'E will."

"The man you're working for?"

Stockton nodded.

"I'd rather be killed b-b-by you than 'im."

Holmes released Stockton.

"If you don't tell me, I'll tell him you did anyway. But if you tell me, he never need know where I got the information."

Stockton looked at us, a crafty smile forming at the corners of his mouth.

"You don't know w-w-what you're talking about," he said. "You don't even know who I'm w-w-working for."

"Oh yes we do," said Holmes.

"You don't," said Stockton, but this time he sounded a little less convinced.

"The dead will rise and the lame will walk," Holmes said suddenly. "He has risen, hasn't he?"

Stockton's face turned as white as his hair.

"'E's the Devil himself," he said in a hoarse whisper. "I wouldn't 'a believed it if I 'adn't s-s-seen it with me own eyes."

Holmes put his face close to Stockton's.

"Why was he so interested in our visit to Mr. Wiggins?"

"All I know is it was s-s-somethin' about a p-p-perfume, somethin' Wiggins w-w-was s'posed to know about."

"That's all you know?"

"Cross me heart; Wiggins died before I c-c-could get any more. I swear it."

Holmes released his grip on Stockton.

"Come on, Watson; we've learned all we're going to from this sewer rat."

"Shouldn't we turn him in for the murder of Mr. Wiggins?" I said.

"There's time for that," Holmes said, walking away. "For the present, he may be more useful to us at large… Besides, once it is discovered that he failed at his task, his life may not be worth much anyway."

We left Stockton trembling and cursing in the street and went back to Baker Street. I lit the fire in the grate and then stood with my back to the fire, thinking. I remembered my friend's words: *Once you have eliminated the impossible, whatever remains, however improbable, is the truth.*

I was, in this case, beginning to redefine what was impossible.

"Can it be, Holmes?" I whispered.

Holmes looked at me, his mouth drawn up in a curious smile.

"Yes, Watson, Professor Moriarty has returned from the dead."

Five

It was some moments before I could think of anything more to say. I realized that even though all the signs had been pointing to that inescapable conclusion, I had somehow not allowed myself to fully believe the fact which now confronted me: *Moriarty lived!*

Holmes lit a cigarette and sat in his chair by the fire. I sank down in the chair opposite him, my head reeling.

"I have been thinking for some time, Watson, that perhaps my old enemy did not die at Reichenbach after all. Incredible as it may seem, it occurred to me relatively soon afterwards that the world might not be rid of him yet."

"But you *saw*–"

"I saw him fall, yes, but I never saw his body–and with a man like Moriarty, more is possible than you would ever think."

"But the chasm–"

"Ah, yes; I can only assume that the drop was not without overhanging ledges. In fact, I was probably remiss in not examining it more carefully at the time. I was somewhat pressed, however; as you know, he had confederates everywhere, and my life was still in danger."

"But what makes you think he's still alive?"

Holmes stared at the picture of Reichenbach Falls which hung on the wall above the mantel.

"For some time I have been seeing signs within the criminal community, certain—*events*—which I was hard put to explain any other way. However, even as the evidence accrued, I refused to believe that such a thing could be true. Even with all of the facts mounting—staring me in the face, as it were—it still seemed impossible; that is, until tonight."

"Tonight? What happened tonight?"

"Several things, actually, although the thing that finally convinced me was Stockton's face."

"His face?"

"I'm not talking about simple fright, Watson. I'm talking about a terror so pure that it is the very distillation of fear: an elemental dread which surpasses all horrors imaginable..." His voice trailed off and the look in his eyes was faraway, distant. "You know I am not easily intimidated, Watson—"

"No, I should say not!"

He looked at me, and there was a vulnerability in his eyes I had never seen before.

"And yet I myself felt that very terror at Reichenbach Falls, there on that ledge with Moriarty." He looked down, and I could see he was in the grip of a strong emotion. "I don't know if there's an English word for it, but the Germans call it *Todesangst,* literally 'death fear.' But it is more than fear of death... it is a fear which is like death in its horror, its power over your very soul." He shuddered, as if attempting to shake off a terrible memory.

"That is what I felt at Reichenbach in those few moments when I struggled with Moriarty, and that is what I saw in Freddie Stockton's eyes tonight. And *that* is why I know he has come back. I don't know how he survived, or what he is trying to do; I only know he has returned."

We sat in silence for some time, listening to the crackle of the wood burning in the grate. There seemed to be nothing else to say.

After a while Holmes got up and lifted the curtain from the window to look down at the street outside. Dusk had fallen, and the sound of horses' hooves upon the cobblestones mingled with the cries of vendors and carriage drivers.

"He is out there somewhere, Watson. He is behind the death of Wiggins, though what he has planned I do not yet know. I shall find out, however, and when I do, no one in London will hide him from me."

I shuddered. After what Holmes had just told me, the thought of actively seeking out Moriarty was more than I could imagine.

"So *he* is the one leaving those messages for you in the *Telegraph*—he is Mr. Fermat?"

"Yes—you may recognize the name, Watson. Pierre de Fermat was a famous mathematician of the seventeenth century. Moriarty is a mathematician himself, and I happen to know he did some work on the proof of Fermat's last theorem, which has never been proven. Hence his choice of the name as an alias."

"What is his game, I wonder?"

"I wonder the same thing, Watson: Why, for example, is he so interested in Miss Merriweather?"

"Miss Merriweather?"

Holmes smiled and cocked his head to one side.

"Oh, yes; surely he knew our visit to Wiggins had something to do with her. Did you not think it an odd coincidence that we should be seated next to her at the concert the other night?"

"I suppose I didn't think about it at all."

"Where did you say you got those two tickets to the concert, Watson?"

"Let me think... oh, yes: They came in the post. There was a thank-you note attached. It was unsigned, but I assumed it was from one of my patients."

"Did you save the envelope?"

"I'm afraid not. It's not uncommon for me to receive such gifts."

"That is unfortunate; it might have contained clues."

"Clues? Are you suggesting that—"

"—that someone wanted us at that concert."

"Moriarty?"

"Or someone else... there may be more than one agent playing this game, Watson."

"Who?"

"I don't know as yet, but I intend to find out."

We were interrupted by the sound of the front doorbell, and I rose to answer it. Holmes was still standing by the window, and he glanced out onto the street.

"Ha! She is back, as I thought she would be."

"Who is back?" I asked, pausing at the door.

"Our friend Miss Merriweather. Would you be so kind as to show her up, Watson?"

"I was just on my way," I answered, bounding down the stairs two at a time. Miss Violet Merriweather was indeed standing in front of the door, and when I opened it she came inside with such hurry that I thought perhaps she was being pursued.

"Oh, Dr. Watson, thank heavens!" she said, trembling, her dark, luminous eyes ringed with fear. A few strands of black hair had escaped the bun at the back of her neck, as though she had dressed in haste.

"What is it, Miss Merriweather?"

Instead of replying, she looked anxiously up the staircase.

"Is Mr. Holmes in?"

"Yes, he is—in fact, he sent me down to bring you up to him."

"Oh, thank heavens!" she said, and headed up the stairs at once.

I followed after her, and before long she was seated in front of the fire, sipping a brandy which Holmes offered her and which she gratefully accepted. Today she wore a powder-blue dress with white lace trim at the throat, and I found myself thinking that it was every bit as becoming as the yellow dress I had last seen her in. I was busy wondering if a dress existed which would not look charming on Miss Merriweather when Holmes interrupted my reverie.

"Now then, Miss Merriweather," he said, "what occasion brings you to call upon my services?"

Miss Merriweather cradled the brandy glass between her hands and looked up at Holmes, her large brown eyes as innocent as a doe's.

"Oh, Mr. Holmes—" Her voice quivered, and I could tell she was about to cry.

I looked at Holmes: On his face was the look of distaste which any display of emotion occasioned. He sat down opposite Miss Merriweather and said gently, "Why don't you begin by telling us exactly what happened the night you left your gloves at the Royal Albert Hall?"

She looked up at him in surprise.

"But how do you know?"

Holmes waved his hand, dismissing the question.

"It was quite obvious you were already in trouble that night, so you might as well start at the beginning and tell me exactly what has transpired."

Holmes' authoritative tone evidently had an effect on Miss Merriweather, for the tears which were threatening to fall suddenly evaporated. She drew herself up in her chair and took a deep breath.

"First I need to know how much you know," she said with dignity. "There is more at stake here than just my honor—"

"Yes, yes; very well," said Holmes impatiently. "I understand you do not want to betray any confidences, least of all *his.*"

At this Miss Merriweather froze, then she looked at me, but when she saw that I had no idea what Holmes was talking about, she laughed—a forced laugh, which came off as a rather pathetic attempt at bravado.

"No doubt you are very clever, Mr. Holmes; at least everyone says you are, but you cannot possibly know—"

"—know which august person has bestowed his favors upon you?" said Holmes smoothly. "My dear Miss Merriweather, what makes you think your secret is so well kept?"

She grew pale at these words, and took another drink of brandy. She could pretend no longer, and looked at Holmes imploringly.

"You *do* know, then," she said quietly.

Holmes poured her some more brandy.

"I shall tell you exactly what I know, Miss Merriweather. For some time now you have been carefully guarding a secret which, if it were to become generally known, would deeply embarrass a great man."

At these words our visitor turned even paler, and lifted the glass of brandy to her lips with shaking hands.

"However, up until now you both have taken great precautions and assumed your secret to be safe. A few days ago, something happened which threatened the very notion of this security: you received a note of blackmail.

"The first payment was to be made at the concert where we first saw you, at the Royal Albert Hall. However, when the messenger did not arrive to pick up the payment at the arranged time, you left in some agitation. Am I correct so far?"

Our visitor shook her head in amazement. "I have heard that you know everything, see everything, Mr. Holmes, and I must say you live up to your reputation."

Holmes continued without acknowledging the compliment.

"I can only assume that your visit here tonight concerns the same delicate matter which you are so anxious to protect. Something else has happened, something with which you feel I may be able to help you. I assume, by the way, that *he* has no idea that you are seeking my services."

Miss Merriweather looked stricken.

"Oh good heavens no, Mr. Holmes—why, he—he would be mortified if he knew I was being blackmailed—I mean—" She stopped, quite flustered.

"Yes, quite," said Holmes. "No doubt you are trying your best to spare him any anxiety at all in the matter."

"Oh, it is essential, Mr. Holmes; I don't what he would do—if his name were dragged into—well, you see my predicament."

"Yes, I do, and your discretion does you credit, Miss Merriweather. By the way, may I assume that your—patron—gave you the very interesting perfume which you are wearing?"

Holmes' words brought a blush to the young lady's cheeks.

"Yes, he did." She turned to me. "You understand, don't you, Dr. Watson, why secrecy is of the utmost importance?"

I was about to say that I certainly *would* understand if I had any idea what they were talking about, but Holmes saved me the trouble.

"I have no secrets from Dr. Watson," he said. "We work together on everything."

"Well, I'm sure you must think me very wicked," she said in a tone which was not entirely ingenuous.

"What I think is not an issue," Holmes replied.

"I can only tell you that I love—and hope that I am loved by—a wonderful man, and if he happens to be a great man, then so be it, but it will not stop me from loving him."

"Your sentiments do you credit, Miss Merriweather," said Holmes, "but really there is no need to justify your actions. I am concerned merely with the matter which now troubles you."

"Very well," said Miss Merriweather, evidently satisfied. "I shall tell you as best I can what has happened these last few days."

"Pray do," said Holmes, sitting across from her in his usual chair, fingertips pressed together, eyes half closed, in his "listening" position.

"Well, I am quite certain that I am being followed," she said. "Ever since the night of the concert there have been two different men lurking outside of my building. No matter what time of day I look out, I always see one or the other, hiding in the shadows of the buildings across the street or loitering about on the pavement."

"Do they know you've spotted them?" Holmes said without opening his eyes.

"I don't think so... I can only assume they followed me here tonight."

"No doubt. Watson, would you be so kind?" said Holmes, motioning me toward the window. I went and lifted the curtain, and, as soon as I did, my eye caught a movement outside. I couldn't be certain, but I think someone stepped back into the shadow of a shop entrance across the street. I let go of the curtain.

"I think I saw your man. I'm not certain, but I think–"

"Thank you, Watson; that will do," said Holmes, sitting up in the chair. "Blackmail is no longer their game. That is, if it ever was."

"What *do* they want from me, then?" she said in an agitated voice.

"Perhaps they want what you are carrying in the inner pocket of your cloak," said Holmes.

Our visitor blanched, and then she laughed again–a forced, mirthless sound.

"Why, Mr. Holmes, whatever do you mean?"

"Miss Merriweather, I would appreciate it if you would drop the pretense," Holmes said impatiently. "If I am going to help you I must insist on complete honesty."

At these words Violet Merriweather's shoulders sagged and her face lost some of its vivacity.

"Very well, Mr. Holmes," she said, rising and fetching her cloak from the rack upon which I had hung it. "I don't know how you could possibly have known—"

"Miss Merriweather, you are a very poor liar. The room is very warm, and yet you parted with your cloak with reluctance when you came in. Since then, you have glanced in the direction of your cloak no less than half a dozen times. Whatever it is you have in there evidently has great value, at least to you."

"I think you will agree that it would have great value to anyone," said Miss Merriweather, extending her hand toward us, palm open.

I do not consider myself a fancier of gemstones, but even I gasped involuntarily when I saw the object in Violet Merriweather's hand. I recognized it at once as a star sapphire, but I had never seen a jewel of such size and luster before. It was as blue and translucent as a tropical sea, and the pattern of a single white star was contained within its depths, catching and reflecting the light in an infinite variety of angles. Indeed, light seemed to emanate from its very core, illuminating everything around it with an unearthly glow. The thing was truly bewitching, and I wanted to gaze at it forever, to plumb the secrets which it contained in its glittering center.

"Pretty, isn't it?" said Holmes, and I could only nod, unable to take my eyes off its radiance.

Holmes turned to Miss Merriweather.

"Well, well, Miss Merriweather," he said, "if I had known you were in possession of *this*... I suppose *he* gave it to you."

"Yes, he did, though I told him it was far too grand a gift."

"I wonder if even he knows how grand it is," murmured Holmes.

"What do you mean?" said our visitor.

"I cannot be absolutely certain, but I think what you now hold in your hand is none other than the Star of India."

This remark produced no impression upon Miss Merriweather, but I was thunderstruck.

"The Star of India!" I exclaimed. "So it *does* exist!"

"What is it?" said Miss Merriweather, puzzled.

"There are tales dating back three centuries which tell of the existence of such a gem," I said. "It was mined—so the story goes—in Ceylon, then purchased and brought to India by an Indian prince as an engagement present for his bride. Soon afterward both of them were murdered, and the gem disappeared, perhaps stolen by whoever killed them. Stories of it have surfaced off and on for years. I myself first heard of it some years ago when I was traveling in the East. I have never doubted that the stone exists, though I never thought I would come face-to-face with it."

"Good heavens—I had no idea!" said Miss Merriweather.

"The superstitions connected with it are legend," said Holmes. "For example, it is said to bring death upon a wrongful owner."

"Perhaps I am better off rid of it, then," Miss Merriweather said with a shudder.

Holmes held out his hand. "May I?"

"Yes, of course."

She handed him the stone and he held it aloft so that it caught the russet glow of the fireplace. It seemed to pull all light into it, like a magnet, and send it back out again magnified a thousand times in beauty and splendor.

"Would you object to leaving this in my safekeeping?" Holmes asked.

Miss Merriweather hesitated, and looked at me with her yielding brown eyes. "No, I suppose not, if you think it would be best."

"I do think so," Holmes replied. "Those who are in pursuit of you may or may not be after this, but I suspect they know you have been given something of great value, and that is why you are being pursued. You will be much safer if you do not have possession of this, at least for now. Miss Merriweather, have you told anyone else other than ourselves of this... situation?"

"No."

"Whatever it is *they* are up to, they are playing a complicated game. You are merely a pawn to them, so I must advise caution on your part. Go nowhere unaccompanied; do not go out at night at all if you can help it, and report to me every day. I will send a young man to check up on you—his name is Tuthill—and you can rely on him to carry a message to me." Holmes rose and put on his coat. "For tonight, I will escort you home. Where do you live?"

"Blackheath. Thank you, Mr. Holmes," she said, rising. "Thank you too, Dr. Watson." A flush of warmth went through my body when she pressed her warm palm to mine. It had been some years since my wife's death and I was unaccustomed to thinking of such things, but I confess that Miss Violet Merriweather had an effect on me.

"Here, Watson—catch," said Holmes, tossing the precious gem at me as though it were a child's toy. "I shan't be long," he said as he closed the door behind him.

I held the stone in my trembling hands, reluctant to put it down. I stood gazing at it for some time, quite entranced. The longer you looked at it, the more all things seemed within your grasp: happiness, love, peace, fulfillment. I told myself that it was a piece of rock, inert matter from the earth, and yet when you looked into its shining depths such realities vanished. I finally placed it carefully upon a cushion on the sideboard and settled down on the couch with my pipe.

The room felt unusually empty. I picked up Miss Merriweather's brandy glass from the table and, in Mrs. Hudson's absence, decided to tidy up. I spent some time arranging things in the room, washing glasses and emptying pipes, all the while thinking of Miss Merriweather's smooth cheeks and full lips. After I finished I sat on the couch and tried to interest myself in a volume of Lord Byron's poetry, but my mind kept wandering to the feeling of that soft hand pressed ever so briefly to mine...

An urgent knocking at the front door shook me out of my reverie. I looked out the window to see who could be calling at such an hour, and was astonished to see a very grand carriage with the royal coat of arms emblazoned on it sitting in front of our building. I smoothed my hair and straightened my collar, and then I hurried down the stairs.

The gentleman who greeted me at the front door was elegantly dressed in a burgundy silk-lined cape and the shiny black boots of a cavalry officer. He was of medium height, with lustrous black hair and a sunburned complexion.

"Dr. Watson, I presume?" His accent was very cultivated, with a suggestion of a foreign tongue.

"Yes," I said, a little awestruck by his grandeur.

"May I come in?"

"Yes, of course." I led the way up the stairs.

"Mr. Holmes is not in at present?" he said after refusing my offer of cognac.

"No, he's gone out. Please sit down, Mr...?"

"Oh, forgive me." He swept aside his cape and sat upon the sofa. "I am Count de Chervaise, Earl of Huntingdon." He shrugged modestly. "It is not as great a title as it sounds. I have, however, been fortunate enough to earn the trust of His Majesty, the Prince–"

"–the Prince of Wales?" I said, scarcely able to believe my ears.

"Yes. We attended school together, and His Majesty is not one to forget services rendered… well, let us just say that he has always been vulnerable to the influence of the weaker sex. In any event, he has sent me on this rather delicate matter for reasons I feel it best not to go into, if you don't mind."

"Yes, of course—I mean, I understand," I said, flustered.

"The matter concerns a gift given to a certain young lady—a gesture made in a moment of passion which was ill-considered, to say the least. The gift was not only monetarily handsome, but it has a political significance which cannot be underestimated. Forgive me if I do not go into the details, but suffice it to say that it could profoundly affect England's relationship with a foreign power…" His eyes roamed the room, and rested on the jewel sitting on the sideboard. "Good heavens!" he said, standing up and taking a step toward it. "Is it possible that—?" He turned to me. "But this is it—this is the very thing I was speaking of! How did you come by it?"

"The young lady in question brought it by not half an hour ago."

"Oh, His Majesty will be pleased!" He rubbed his elegant hands together. "He had feared… well, you see the delicacy of the situation. And here it is! You will let me return it to him, won't you?"

"Well, it was given to us—to Mr. Holmes, really—for safekeeping."

"Yes, yes; of course, and Mr. Holmes shall receive His Majesty's personal thanks for his part in the matter."

"But the young lady—"

"Yes, well, it can't be helped," said the count, shrugging his shoulders. "As I said, His Majesty acted unwisely, but I'm sure you yourself know what the throes of love can do to a man."

"Well, certainly, but—"

"Then we shall say no more upon the subject." He reached for the jewel, but I stepped in front of him.

"I'm sorry, but you will have to wait for my friend Sherlock Holmes to return. I cannot allow you to—"

He made a quick movement with his right hand, and I felt the hard barrel of a revolver pressed into my ribs.

"Forgive me, Dr. Watson. I had hoped not to resort to such... well, crude behavior. Still, it can't be helped," he said, plucking the jewel from where it lay and depositing it into a silken pouch which hung from his belt. "Good night, Dr. Watson, and thank you for your invaluable assistance."

With a bow and a flourish of his cape, he was gone. As soon as I heard the click of the front door latch I bounded down the stairs after him. I arrived in the street just in time to watch his carriage drive off into the night. I looked around for a cab, hoping to follow him, but none was forthcoming, and after several minutes I gave up and trudged dejectedly back upstairs.

I sat down to await Holmes' return. My heart felt heavy as a stone in my chest, beating dully against my ribs. I could still feel the place where the gun had pressed against those ribs, but I blamed myself, thinking that if only I had not been taken so off guard I could have prevented this. After another quarter of an hour I heard Holmes' light step upon the stairs, and I opened the door to let him in.

"Ah, Watson, you needn't have waited up." He hung up his coat and went to warm himself by the fire. "Where did you put it, by the way?"

My heart sank. "Holmes," I began, but my voice gave me away. He looked at me intently.

"What has happened?" he said softly.

I explained everything, and he sat listening, asking questions about the coat of arms on the carriage, the man's clothing, and other details. When I had finished he sat for a moment without saying anything. I felt as bad as I ever had before in my life. I could think of nothing to say, and stood miserably, waiting to be castigated for my stupidity. To my surprise, however, when Holmes spoke his voice was gentle.

"It's my fault, really," he said. "I left in too great a hurry, and it didn't occur to me that he would make his move so quickly. He was obviously ready for us, and had several plans waiting to be put into action. I should have warned you; really I should have. Don't blame yourself, Watson."

The kinder his words were, the more I did blame myself, of course. I had failed Miss Merriweather and the Prince of Wales, but most of all I had failed Holmes.

"Holmes, I—" I began. Holmes put his hand on my shoulder.

"Never mind, Watson; it's better that you didn't put up a struggle. He most certainly wouldn't have hesitated to shoot you. What did you say the man looked like?"

"Well, he was not much taller than me, though very grand and elegant, with a trace of a foreign accent of some kind. His hair was very black and his skin was quite dark."

"He was dark, you say? Could he perhaps be of Indian descent?"

"I suppose so, although his accent suggested he was educated at an English university."

Holmes rubbed his forehead. "Hmm... I'm not aware of anyone of that description moving in London criminal circles. Still, Moriarty's web stretches far and wide, and it is not difficult to imagine that he could have such a man working for him. Never mind, Watson," he said, seeing my glum face. "Now all that matters is what to do next. It's too late to act tonight, so I suggest we both get some rest. If you'd care to stay here tonight, I would feel better about your safety."

"Well, I—" I began, but Holmes interrupted me.

"I do think it would be safer for you not to venture out tonight."

I nodded, still feeling terribly guilty. "Very well, if you think so."

"I do."

I took his advice and went to bed, though I doubt if either of us slept much that night. I tossed and turned fitfully, dreaming of the sound of coach wheels against cobblestone in the night and midnight jewels reflecting in candlelight.

Six

I awoke to the smell of coffee. I could tell by the height of the pale autumn sun that it was late. Thinking Holmes had no doubt been up for hours, I went downstairs, only to see the table set and Mrs. Hudson pouring coffee.

"Mrs. Hudson! I thought you were in Cornwall for another week."

"I decided to cut my holiday short. Mr. Holmes needs me more than my sister does right now," she said gruffly, though I knew the affection underlying her words.

"I can't argue with that," I said, sitting at the table. "Where is he, by the way?"

"He's gone out," she replied, pouring me a cup of coffee. "Now, how do you want your eggs?"

"I'm not very hungry," I said moodily.

"Now, Dr. Watson, there's no need to punish me or yourself for your mistake," Mrs. Hudson said sternly.

"Holmes told you, did he?" I said, still feeling sulky.

"Yes, he did, and it could have happened to anyone. Now, how do you want your eggs?"

I suddenly had to laugh. "It's good to have you back, Mrs. Hudson."

"I don't see what's so funny about it," she said, and trundled off to the kitchen.

After breakfast I rummaged around the room, looking for something which might tell me where Holmes had gone. Sitting on the couch was a copy of that morning's *Telegraph,* opened to the classified. I scanned it eagerly for another entry from the ubiquitous Mr. Fermat, and I was soon rewarded. "From Mr. Fermat to Mr. Shomel," it read. "My knight has gained ground but I have left my rook unprotected."

I put down the paper and pondered these words. I could make neither head nor tail of it, though I have no doubt the meaning was clear to Holmes and Moriarty. As I was trying to unravel the meaning, Mrs. Hudson entered the room.

"Inspector Lestrade to see you, sir. Shall I show him in?"

"Yes, thank you, Mrs. Hudson."

Inspector Lestrade of Scotland Yard was a slight man who wore his vanity uneasily, like an ill-fitting suit. The impression was of a man who wasn't sure whether or not he really believed his own presentation of himself. He was given to huffiness, easily insulted, and more than a little pompous. Like so many people, he was intimidated by Sherlock Holmes' superior intelligence, and resented the fact that he had so often needed the great detective's help in solving his cases. Nonetheless, there was something touching about the man, a certain childlike innocence in his ferret-like face.

He entered the room and when he saw I was alone his face expressed disappointment mingled with unmistakable relief.

"So Mr. Holmes isn't here?" he said.

"No, I'm afraid not. Can I help you, Inspector?"

Lestrade sat wearily on the couch.

"I'll just wait here for Mr. Holmes, if that's all right with you. What time do you expect him back?"

"I really can't say. I don't even know where he went."

Lestrade sighed and twisted his hat in his hands.

"It's a bloody nuisance," he muttered, and I didn't know if he meant Holmes' absence or the matter Lestrade had come to see him about. There was a pause and then he said, "I got a message from Mr. Holmes last night regarding the death of that poor deformed chap he knew—"

"Oh, yes, Wiggins."

"Nasty piece of business, that... looks like he was strangled. How was it Mr. Holmes knew about it?"

I wasn't sure what Holmes had told Lestrade, so I deflected his question.

"Oh, you know Holmes—there's very little that goes on in London that he doesn't know about."

I said nothing about his theory regarding the return of Professor Moriarty, feeling that the divulgence of such information was best left to Holmes himself. Right now I wasn't even sure I believed it myself. In the light of day—even a gray London day—it seemed only a remote possibility.

Lestrade picked up the Persian slipper which held Holmes' tobacco, looked at it, put it back down on the table, and sighed deeply.

"Would you like something to drink?" I said.

He looked at me hopefully. "Thanks all the same, but it's a little early for that, don't you think?"

"I meant tea or something."

His face fell. "Oh, right; of course—tea would be very nice, thank you," he said unconvincingly.

"I'll just see to it with Mrs. Hudson," I said, and left him to his own devices for a few minutes while I consulted with Mrs. Hudson. She was in her kitchen, sleeves rolled up to her elbows, pounding away at some pastry dough, flour flying in all directions.

"Yes, yes—I'll get to it right away," she said when I made my request for tea. I was suddenly so happy to see her safe and sound at Baker Street once again that I had an impulse to kiss her on the cheek. When I did, she looked at me with a startled expression. "*Really,* Dr. Watson," she said, flustered, but I could tell she was pleased.

When I returned to the sitting room Lestrade was pacing the floor restlessly. "This came for you while you were downstairs," he said, handing me an elegant, cream-colored envelope. It was addressed to Holmes and bore the letterhead of the Diogenes Club.

"Isn't that the name of his brother's club?" said Lestrade. "You know, that place for strange fellows who go there to avoid talking to one another?"

"Yes, it is," I answered, tucking the envelope into my jacket pocket.

"Right; I thought so. It's a bit odd, a place like that, if you ask me… but then the more you work at a job like mine the more everything begins to look odd after a while. What's his brother's name again?"

"Mycroft."

"Right. What's he up to these days?"

"Well, I don't know. Holmes says he is a creature of habit. He rarely speaks of his brother."

"Strange, that, with both of them living here in London, don't you think?" Lestrade gave a dry little laugh. "But I suppose Mr. Holmes isn't exactly what you'd call a family man, eh?"

"No, I suppose not."

Mrs. Hudson entered with the tea, and Lestrade tucked into the plate of Scottish shortbread with gusto.

"Not bad, these," he said, his mouth full of crumbs. "I believe Mr.

Holmes once told me his brother was involved in the government in some way."

To say that Mycroft Holmes was "involved in the government" was like saying that the ocean was "involved in water." Sherlock Holmes— not a man given to overstatement—had once told me that Mycroft *was* the government. According to Holmes, his brother's capacious mind consolidated and coordinated policies of all the various departments, and that very little happened at a national level without the input of Mycroft Holmes. He was like a giant reasoning machine sitting at the very center of government, which turned slowly round him like a wheel on its axis.

Lestrade and I made our way to the bottom of the teapot and through a second plate of shortbread. Finally Lestrade stood up and brushed the crumbs from his trousers.

"Well, Dr. Watson, I'd best be going now. Tell Mr. Holmes, if you would, that I came by. I'm afraid I don't have much news about the case. My boys are out trying to find that Stockton fellow that Mr. Holmes says is involved, but it's as though he's disappeared into thin air. Also, we brought that parrot over to the Yard. Mr. Holmes seems to think there's something to what the bird says, though to me it sounds just like idle chattering." He took another gulp of tea, set his cup down, and put on his coat wearily.

"Well, thank you for the tea, Dr. Watson, and I'd appreciate it if you'd ask Mr. Holmes to contact me if he has any more information."

"I will, Inspector."

Lestrade had not been gone long when the door burst open and Holmes entered. His face was cut and bleeding, and he was holding his left arm.

"Holmes!" I said, rising from my chair.

"Steady on, Watson; I'm all right," he said, though he didn't look it.

"What happened, Holmes?"

He walked somewhat unsteadily to the fireplace and sank down in his usual chair.

"I managed to play the part of the hound but I got a bit stuck in the role of the fox at the end. No matter, though—I found out what I needed to know."

"Where have you been?"

Instead of answering, Holmes glanced at the copy of the *Telegraph* which still lay open upon the table.

"Ah, I see you have been doing a bit of sleuthing on your own, Watson—"

"Never mind about me; what happened to you?"

"Well, since you evidently have read the entry from Mr. Fermat, I should think you might deduce, Watson."

"Holmes, this is no time for games," I said, fetching my medical kit from the corner. "Would you *please* just tell me—"

"Very well," Holmes said a bit huffily, "if you insist. I supposed that whatever Moriarty had in mind, he was luring me into a trap of some sort; the trick was in sensing it ahead of time and acting accordingly."

"You could have at least taken me with you," I said, hurt at being excluded.

"There was no time," Holmes replied. "That can wait, Watson," he said in response to my attempt to clean his wounds.

"No, it *can't* wait; I will do it now," I said with unaccustomed force, whereupon Holmes shrugged and submitted to my ministrations. "Whatever it was he had planned, it evidently worked to some degree," I said as I applied iodine to the cuts and bruises on Holmes' face.

"Moriarty's fatal flaw is his vanity, Watson, his intellectual arrogance. He could have misled me entirely, but he could not resist putting the solution just within my grasp, for the sport of it." Holmes lifted the newspaper from the table. "You see, in deciphering this message, there were many potential meanings, for a rook is both a castle and a type of bird."

"Yes, so it is."

"However, it is also slang for a swindler, or one who cheats at gambling. I happen to know that one of Moriarty's agents–George Simpson, remember? In all likelihood, it was he who kidnapped Mrs. Hudson–"

"Yes, I remember. Hold still, please."

"Well, this Simpson is an inveterate gambler. In fact, it is his constantly accruing gambling debts which keep him in thrall to Moriarty. In any event, I know that Moriarty does not like to keep anyone in his confidence, but that Simpson comes as close as anybody to being his right-hand man, so to speak. Therefore, I concluded that Simpson is the rook referred to in the cryptic message. So I decided to pay a visit to Mr. Simpson at his favorite gaming establishment." Holmes winced as the iodine stung his abrasions. "They often gamble through the night, and I arrived just as the game was breaking up."

"And what did you hope to find there?"

"Exactly what I did find, Watson: Moriarty's next move."

"And what is that?"

"Well, I persuaded Mr. Simpson through the rather crude use of fisticuffs to reveal a key bit of information: The theft of the jewel is part of a larger blackmail plan–"

"Oh, that reminds me: Inspector Lestrade was here earlier."

"Oh, yes; I tipped him off about Stockton being behind Wiggins' murder."

"Oh, and this came for you," I said a little sheepishly, suddenly remembering the note from the Diogenes Club. I took it from my jacket and handed it to Holmes, who opened it eagerly and read it.

"So," he said after a moment, "they have come to Mycroft for help. Things must be dire indeed, because now Mycroft has come to me."

Holmes folded the note and put it in his pocket.

"By the way, did you tell Lestrade of Moriarty's reappearance?"

"No, I thought I would leave that to you. To be honest, I doubted whether he would believe me."

"Perhaps you're right," said Holmes. "It's ironic, isn't it? His resurrection, as it were, is almost biblical. Instead of Christ who's risen this time, though, it's Satan who has risen after the Fall. Do you know your Milton, Watson?"

"It's a bit rusty, perhaps, but I did read him in school," I said.

> "'The mind is its own place, and in itself
> Can make a Heav'n of Hell, a Hell of Heav'n.'

"Moriarty lives in his own private hell, Watson, and he has spent his life trying to bring others into it with him, because one can get lonely in hell."

I thought this was rather uncharacteristically philosophical of Holmes, and I said so. He shrugged.

"Perhaps so. But I have had many years to think about this, Watson, and I hope you will indulge me in a little philosophizing."

"Certainly, Holmes; certainly."

He rose somewhat stiffly from his chair.

"I think a bit of late lunch at the Cafe Royal is in order, and then we will pay a visit on my brother."

Seven

Mycroft Holmes was such a creature of habit that you could set your watch by him. His routine was sacred, and it never varied: He spent the day at his office in Whitehall and then at exactly 4:45 he made his way to the Diogenes Club, where he was to be found until 7:40. The club is just opposite his rooms on Pall Mall, and it was to this august establishment that Holmes and I made our way after fortifying ourselves with the grilled lamb at the Cafe Royal. Holmes ate as though he hadn't eaten all day, which I have no doubt was the case.

It was exactly 5:57 when we entered the Diogenes Club, that extraordinary establishment where London's most antisocial men gather to indulge in their mutual need for seclusion. It had been some time since I had been to the Diogenes, and yet, as soon as Holmes and I entered the front hall, I remembered our first visit there some years ago. Nothing had changed. There was the same tomblike silence in the front hallway, the same elegant glass paneling through which I could see the large and comfortable reading room. I even fancied that the very same men were sitting in leather armchairs reading their papers. I followed

Holmes into a small antechamber looking out over Pall Mall. The room smelled of ancient leather and books.

"If you would wait here just a moment, I shall return," he said in a whisper.

I nodded and sat myself upon a large Turkish cushion which covered the window seat. Apart from the noise coming from the street, the only sound I could hear was the steady ticking of the grandfather clock in the lobby. The place had a mummified air, as though time did not exist inside its thick stone walls. I could almost believe that the inhabitants themselves did not age so long as they sat in their stuffed armchairs, immobile and silent except for the occasional crackle of a page turning.

Holmes returned with his brother Mycroft. He was exactly as I had remembered him, only perhaps a little thicker around his considerable girth. He extended his hand to me, and his gray eyes crinkled warmly.

"Dr. Watson, so nice to see you again. I would say the same to you, Sherlock, but I must say you look as though you've just emerged from a brawl," he added, looking at Holmes' bruised face.

Holmes dismissed the comment with an impatient wave of his hand.

"The fact is it's a delicate matter, a piece of tricky business," Mycroft continued. "A matter of international relations, you might say." He cleared his throat and looked around the room, as though he were afraid of being overheard. There was no sound of any kind coming from the hollow stone corridors, but he lowered his voice all the same.

"It seems that a particular Indian prince was in possession of a jewel which was supposed to confer great favor upon its owner.

"The Star of India," said Holmes. Mycroft regarded him through narrowed eyes. "So you're involved already," he said. "Why didn't you tell me?"

Holmes shrugged. "I'm telling you now."

"Well, never mind. Let me tell you what I know first. This same Indian prince gives the Star of India to the Prince of Wales as a gesture of friendship. And now this Indian prince is coming to London next week, and he's made it clear that he expects to see his gift displayed among the Crown jewels—which is fine until the jewel goes missing. It's gone, and no one knows who took it."

Mycroft extracted a piece of paper from his jacket pocket and handed it to Holmes.

"This morning the Minister of Foreign Affairs received this message. That is when they contacted me. If the jewel is not recovered it's likely to touch off an international situation."

I looked over Holmes' shoulder at the paper, trying to employ my friend's methods in analyzing it. The message was handwritten in block letters on plain parchment which was a dark shade of ivory. When I looked at the watermark I saw that it was a common one available in most stationery stores. The ink was black, and I would have said the lettering belonged to a person of great force of personality.

"The Star of India is in my keeping," it read, "until such time as my demands can be met by the government. I will send you my first demand within twenty-four hours."

"This is not good, Sherlock—not good at all," Mycroft Holmes said, frowning.

"No," answered Holmes. "What is the name of this Indian prince, by the way?"

"Prince Chandan Tagore Rabarrath. You see, Prince Rabarrath represents a significant segment of his people, and they are on the verge of declaring warfare on another group within India. Prince Rabarrath has considerable influence; he currently has the largest following of any leader in India. Unfortunately, there are a number of extremist elements among his followers, and it is very important that we maintain a good relationship with him. The political unrest in that country is considerable; not only are there groups agitating for the removal of English rule, but there is also the threat of civil and religious warfare within India."

"I see," said Holmes, and began telling Mycroft everything that had happened to us in the past few days. When he came to the part about the stone conferring good fortune upon its owner, Mycroft interrupted.

"Upon its *rightful* owner," he said, smiling. "Like most superstitious beliefs, there is a dark side to this one: unworthy or unlawful owners of the stone are supposedly cursed–and we believe that certain sects within Prince Rabarrath's people would feel compelled to commit certain violent acts to make sure that the curse is borne out."

"This is very serious indeed," said Holmes.

"Yes, it is. I'm glad that you are involved, Sherlock."

"Thank you for your confidence, Mycroft, but I feel I must tell you that–"

"–that *he* has returned?"

Holmes stared at his brother.

"How did you know?"

Mycroft waved the question away with a hand so fat that it was more like the flipper of a seal. "Really, Sherlock, you do me some insult by looking so astonished. It is true that I am not so energetic as yourself, but like you I do not merely see, I *observe*. In fact, I am quite certain we have come to the same conclusion: that *he* is behind all of this in some way. Am I right?"

"You are," said Holmes in a low voice. "But why didn't you tell me?"

"For the simple reason that, like yourself, I had only suspicions–until now, that is. There are aspects of this case which are so clearly the work of his hand that one can really come to no other conclusion."

"Yes, exactly what I thought."

Mycroft sighed and took another paper from his breast pocket; without a word he handed it to his brother. Holmes read it and gave it back.

"So this is his game," he said grimly.

"What is it?" I said, feeling somewhat of a third wheel between the two brilliant brothers.

"A demand for money from the Exchequer in exchange for the Star of India."

"Good heavens."

"Well, if he is playing a game of such stakes you would expect him to ask such a reward; if you play a high-risk game you expect the odds to pay off."

Holmes sank into his chair and stared out the window which overlooked Pall Mall. Well-dressed men and women came and went, part of the endless procession of humanity which is London. "It is all a game to him on some level," Holmes said moodily, "just a game…" Suddenly he sat bolt upright in his chair. "That's it—a game! We must not neglect that aspect, for therein lies the key!"

"What are you talking about, Sherlock?" said Mycroft Holmes.

"Chess, my dear Mycroft—the board game of warfare."

"What's that got to do with Moriarty?"

"I was about to tell you when you interrupted me earlier," Holmes replied. He then told Mycroft about the chess references which Moriarty had been placing in the *Telegraph*.

"If I am not mistaken—" began Holmes.

"—and you seldom are—" Mycroft interjected dryly.

"—I believe the term *exchequer* is from the Latin *saccarium,* or chessboard."

"You are correct," said Mycroft. "Roman accounts of revenue were kept on a squared board, much like a chessboard; hence the derivation."

"There is something here," said Holmes, rising from his chair and pacing about the room. "It only needs figuring out."

"For God's sake, Sherlock, stop that infernal pacing; you are making me quite nervous."

Holmes stopped and looked at his corpulent older brother, so unlike himself physically and yet so similar mentally. His expression was something close to affection, though if I had remarked upon it he would have promptly denied it.

"You never could stand excess movement of any kind, could you, Mycroft?" he said.

Mycroft shrugged his massive shoulders. "I dislike waste of any kind, Sherlock, either mental or physical; excessive expenditure of energy has always seemed to me to be an abuse of Nature."

Holmes smiled and sat down again, but his long fingers twitched nervously upon the arms of his chair.

"There is a woman involved, of course," Mycroft said.

I stared at him. "How did you know that?"

He chuckled, a deep rumbling sound which came from the folds of flesh at his throat.

"My dear Dr. Watson, there is *always* a woman involved, sooner or later—especially when priceless jewels are at stake. In fact, I have people checking on her background as we speak."

"And what have they found?" said Holmes.

"Nothing, as yet. She has been at her present address for only a few months, and so far the post office hasn't come up with any previous listings for her. We're somewhat hampered by the need to make our inquiries discreetly, of course, so it is proceeding slowly."

"Do you suspect her, then?" I said, my heart sinking.

Mycroft shrugged and twisted the gold signet ring he wore on his right hand. "I would suspect her were she Caesar's wife herself."

"I'm afraid my brother shares my jaundiced view of the 'weaker sex,' as they are so mistakenly called," said Holmes.

"The more his loss," I muttered.

"Oh come now, Watson, don't sulk," said Holmes. "Just because you are a bit taken with the young lady in question, there's no reason to get moody."

I could feel my face redden.

"I am not–"

Holmes put a hand on my shoulder.

"Forgive me; I didn't mean to embarrass you. It wasn't a criticism– she is a most attractive young lady."

"I didn't think you noticed these things about women," I said.

Mycroft laughed. "Oh, that is what he has always pretended. He notices everything, as I do; it's simply a question of whether one acts upon it or not. I myself seldom act on anything."

"True," said his brother. "I was reading an extraordinary tale the other day, by Herman Melville–"

"–the American writer?"

"Yes, the same. The main character reminded me of you in some ways. His name was Bartleby."

Mycroft Holmes smiled. "I have read it. He more or less starves to death, I believe. There is no fear of that where I am concerned," he said, patting his substantial middle. "On the other hand, you are looking a bit thin, Sherlock," he said, studying his brother's lean form. "Has he been eating, Dr. Watson?"

"Well, I doubt that he ate much while Mrs. Hudson was away, but now she's returned."

"Good. I doubt Moriarty has any further use for her. He certainly is planning his moves ahead, exactly as you might on a chessboard..."

Holmes sprang from his chair.

"I have it!" he cried. "It isn't the Exchequer which is his chessboard! Mycroft, is there a map of London anywhere in this building?"

"I believe there are some maps in the large oak desk in the reading room."

"Watson, would you be so kind as to fetch it for me?" said Holmes.

"Yes, certainly," I said, intrigued.

"You'll find them in the top drawer, I believe," Mycroft said to me, and then he turned to his brother. "I think I see where you are heading with this, Sherlock... clever, very clever."

I left the two brothers talking in low, urgent tones, their bowed heads almost touching, and headed for the large sitting room I had seen when we first entered the club. My footsteps clattered noisily upon the hard wood floor of the connecting hallway, and I anticipated annoyed looks from the denizens of that stately chamber. However, upon entering it, I was virtually ignored. Except for an old colonel with a weather-lined face who glanced at me over his spectacles, no one paid me any attention.

I tiptoed across the thick Persian carpet and opened the top drawer of the heavy oak desk which sat along the far wall. The drawer was practically empty save for several dog-eared maps of London. I chose the least dilapidated one and tiptoed back to where Holmes and his brother awaited me.

"Well done, Watson!" Holmes cried, seizing the map from me as soon as I entered. He spread the map out upon the small low coffee table which sat in front of us. Producing a pen from his pocket, he drew a square around the city. Within the square he drew a grid of crisscrossed lines so that the effect was one of a chessboard superimposed over the city of London.

"You see: Here is your chessboard!" he cried triumphantly.

Mycroft Holmes studied the map with interest.

"So you think he is essentially playing an elaborate game of chess?" I asked.

"Indeed I do. At first I thought he was just playing with the metaphorical implications, but now... well, you see how the Thames intersects London almost exactly in half? If you regard the northern half of the city as our side, and the southern half as his territory, you have a rough model for a chess game."

"Very interesting, Sherlock," said Mycroft. "I think you have something here."

"He made his first move here," Holmes said, drawing an X behind St. Paul's Church in Covent Garden, where Wiggins' perfume shop was located.

"But what about Mrs. Hudson?" I said. "First he had her kidnapped—"

"That was merely an exercise; he just wanted to remove us from the board while he made his real first move, which resulted in poor Wiggins' death. We countered when we got information out of Freddie Stockton," he continued, drawing another X in the neighborhood of Lambeth. "His next attack was to send his 'knight' up to Baker Street to capture the jewel. This morning when I wrung information out of Simpson I was literally counter-attacking."

"And that was where?" said Mycroft.

"Here, in Southwark," said Holmes, drawing an X over that notorious neighborhood, well known for its criminal slums.

"Well, I congratulate you, Sherlock," said his brother, "and I must say, it is most ingenious."

"We must endeavor at all times to be at least one or two moves ahead of him. Mycroft, I believe you have some expertise in chess—I recall you displayed a certain gift for the game as a child. Have you kept up your interest?"

Mycroft shrugged his broad shoulders. "Not entirely. I still play the occasional game, but I am hardly an expert. I found it valuable mostly as a form of mental training. I am not attracted to games in general, and, as you know, you often beat me. However, with some study, I could regain some of my skill in time–"

"We don't *have* any time!" cried Holmes. "That is the one thing we *don't* have!"

"Sherlock, please lower your voice," said Mycroft, looking over his shoulder into the silent halls. "You have no idea how annoying noise of any kind is to the gentlemen here."

Holmes did not reply, and began pacing the room like a caged tiger. Mycroft and I watched in silence for a few moments, and then Holmes abruptly stopped and threw himself into one of the armchairs.

"Never mind; it will have to do," he said, his hands twitching upon the armrests, "that is, if you're game," he added, looking at his brother sternly.

Mycroft Holmes sighed. "I don't see that I have a choice. I just hope it doesn't involve too much rushing around; you know how I hate to disturb my routine."

"Leave the rushing around to me," said Holmes. "All I require from you is some expertise in the game of chess. Oh, by the way, I may need the assistance of Scotland Yard. How much is safe to tell them?"

Mycroft shrugged his plump shoulders. "Whatever is necessary to get the help you need. I wouldn't go around broadcasting information, though–not to those street arabs of yours, at any rate."

Holmes dismissed the last remark with an impatient wave of his hand. "Just because you have an aversion to children, Mycroft, is no reason to cast aspersions on my associates. I can assure you Master Tuthill and his friends are of great use to me."

It was Mycroft's turn to be impatient, and I was amused to see him use the exact same gesture as his brother: a backwards wave of the hand, as if swatting away flies.

"There is only one thing that concerns me," Mycroft said. "When Moriarty strikes, he doesn't hesitate to actually remove your players from the board, as in the case of poor Mr. Wiggins... I wonder, are you prepared to do the same?"

Holmes looked out the window onto the bustling streets of Pall Mall, his face grim in the dull gray light.

"I don't know," he said softly. "I suppose I'll do whatever I have to do..." He then shuddered and shook himself as if to rid himself of the black mood which threatened to settle over all of us.

"Well, I shall do my best, though I can't guarantee anything," said Mycroft, rising from the depths of his armchair like a whale rising from the depths of the sea. "I'll tell you one thing, though, Sherlock: One way or another he must be stopped. The world is not safe with him about and operating freely."

"Yes," said Holmes, looking at his brother, "no one knows that better than I do."

Eight

We accepted Mycroft Holmes' invitation to join him in a light late supper at his club.

"The chef isn't bad—he's Belgian, you know, which is almost as good as being French," he whispered as we were shown to a quiet table in the corner, next to a French window covered by heavy crimson brocade drapes. The smells coming from the kitchen were inviting; I could detect the aroma of roasting meat and fresh butter. The dining room was nearly deserted, and the waiters came and went quietly, making scarcely any noise at all. I suspected that one of the qualifications for employment at the Diogenes Club was the ability to be silent, and imagined the manager enjoining his staff to tiptoe about so as not to disturb the peculiar clientele.

However, talking was not forbidden in the dining room, and Holmes spent the entire meal talking about the game of chess with his brother. I listened as the brothers discussed various common attack strategies, as well as a few not quite so well known. Holmes sat, his eyes transfixed upon the graph of a chessboard which Mycroft had sketched upon a piece of paper. I barely said a dozen words myself during the entire meal, preferring instead to play the part of the child who sits quietly in the corner while his elders discuss the affairs of the world. Indeed, I felt like hardly more than a child in the presence of these two brothers with their magnificent brains. While it is true that my own mental gifts included a modest ability to spin a narrative or turn a phrase, I felt distinctly inferior to these two intellectual titans, and was content to sit and listen to their exchange.

"I can't say that I see any conventional patterns in Moriarty's strategy as yet," said Mycroft Holmes as he helped himself to more salmon en croûte. "Several things are clear, though: For example, the man who took the Star of India from Dr. Watson is evidently moving as a knight—"

"—because he 'jumped over' Watson in order to make his move, I presume," said Holmes.

"Precisely. The knight is the most curious traveler of all, particularly in his ability to jump over other players in order to make a capture."

I didn't much like the idea of being "jumped over" by anyone—much less one of Moriarty's confederates—but I said nothing.

"However," Mycroft continued, cutting himself a thick slice of pâté de campagne, "there is one thing which is absolutely essential to remember: A careful player always studies his opponent's moves as thoroughly as his own. Not to do so is to invite disaster. A brilliant attack will sometimes succeed before either side has lost many men, but most evenly matched games are won by an accumulation of small successes which weaken the enemy. Even if one is on the defensive, it is better to have a definite plan of attack… the next move is his, I believe, is it not?"

"Yes."

"You must try to anticipate what that might be; in other words, you must endeavor to think like your enemy."

Holmes nodded, his gray eyes ablaze with an inner fire.

"I have already come to the same conclusion. The only way to defeat such an antagonist is to put yourself in his place. I shall have to train myself to think like Moriarty."

Mycroft Holmes and I exchanged glances; we both knew the threat such a challenge could pose to his brother's physical and mental health. Even now the strain on his nerves was beginning to show; his face looked haggard and drawn, and his fingers twitched incessantly upon the white tablecloth.

As we left the Diogenes Club, Mycroft Holmes pulled me aside.

"Look after him, Dr. Watson," he said in a low voice. "The danger to all of us is great, but it is greatest to him."

"You can rely upon me," I said, though my voice expressed a confidence I did not feel.

Holmes was unusually quiet on the way back to Baker Street. Upon entering his rooms he went directly to the shelf containing his reference books and pulled out a volume of the *Encyclopaedia Britannica*.

"Let us see what they have to say about the game of chess," he said, leafing through the pages. "This is curious," he said after he had read for some moments. "Did you know that the game was invented in the Far East, most probably India?"

"I believe I once heard something to that effect. It is centuries old, is it not?"

"Yes, just like the Star of India… curious, how all roads in this affair seem to lead to India."

"It could be just coincidence. After all, it is a rich and ancient culture."

"Coincidence, Watson, is often just a lazy man's view of a pattern. Listen to this: The word *chess* is supposedly derived from *shah*–the Persian word for king–and *checkmate* from *shah mat,* meaning 'the king is dead.'" He looked up at me. "You realize, of course, what that means?"

I nodded. "The Prince himself may be in danger."

"I am afraid so. The possibility certainly exists, and we must proceed accordingly... I wonder, does he really intend to try something so outrageous, and if so, what does he hope to gain?"

"I don't know, Holmes," I said, looking at my watch, "but it's late, and you can't have gotten very much sleep last night. I know *I* didn't—"

"You go on ahead to bed, Watson, and I'll follow later," he said, selecting a meerschaum pipe from the pipe rack over the mantel. "I have a few things to ponder."

"Very well, Holmes, but don't be up too late—it isn't good for you, you know."

"Yes, yes, I know," he said, but already I could tell his mind had turned to other things. He sat in his usual armchair, his legs tucked up under him, filling his pipe with shag tobacco, a pensive look on his face. I sighed and trudged up the stairs to bed; he would no doubt be up for hours. Holmes would always be Holmes, and there was nothing I could do to change that.

I slept somewhat more soundly that night, though I was awakened by a cold dawn which pressed through my window shades and fell, bleak and cheerless, upon the bedroom carpet, draining it of all its color. There are few things as dreary as a London dawn in October, and I watched the gathering gray light for a while, then slipped off into a fitful sleep, until I was awakened by the smell of coffee.

"Well, Watson, I was beginning to wonder if we would number you among the living today," Holmes said cheerfully as I stumbled down the stairs, rubbing my eyes. "I trust you slept well?"

"Yes, thank you," I replied, annoyed at his superior attitude. He looked hale enough, though the dark circles around his eyes suggested that his own rest had been minimal. I was pleased to see that he was attacking his breakfast with gusto, and I followed suit, tucking into Mrs. Hudson's kippers with a keen appetite.

"As soon as you've finished I thought we would go over to Scotland Yard," said Holmes.

"Oh?"

"That is, I would be pleased to have you accompany me if you can spare the time. There are one or two little matters I need to see Lestrade about."

I nodded, my mouth full of kippers. "Of course; I'll just stop by my surgery to see how McKinney is getting along. He's been filling in for me the past few days."

"Yes, so you said."

"Then I'll come along and meet you there, if that's all right."

"Perfectly. The good inspector may have one or two questions that you may be able to answer better than I—matters involving poor Wiggins' death and the like."

We agreed to meet in an hour or so at the Yard, and I went along to my surgery to see how McKinney was doing. He was a competent young chap, not long out of medical school at Edinburgh. He had filled in for me before, and I had every confidence that he could handle things in my absence.

When I arrived, McKinney was seeing a patient, so I sat in the waiting room and looked through my mail. A plain envelope with no return address and no postage caught my eye, and when I opened it I found inside a single sheet of paper; upon it was written simply "K.Kt.-B4," in large block letters. I was pondering the meaning of this cryptic message when Dr. McKinney came in from the office to greet me. He was a tall, handsome Scot with a long Celtic face and stiff, curly hair the color of toasted straw.

"This envelope—when did it arrive?" I said.

"Oh, funny you should ask," McKinney replied. "It was delivered by a strange little fellow with ginger muttonchops just a few minutes ago. He didn't speak at all, just handed it to me and left."

I was struck immediately by the thought that this was the same little man who had thrust the newspaper into my hands at Waterloo Station. I now had the uncomfortable sensation that I was being followed. I said nothing to McKinney, however, but shoved the paper into my pocket. We talked for a quarter of an hour about various matters concerning my practice, patients, bills, and the like, during which time I completely forgot about the paper in my pocket. I went over several of the cases with Dr. McKinney and then left my surgery, heading straight for Scotland Yard.

When I arrived I was shown to Lestrade's office, and the door was opened by none other than Sherlock Holmes himself.

"Come in, Watson! You're just in time to help me recount to Lestrade here the events surrounding Wiggins' murder."

I entered the office, and saw immediately that the room had another occupant apart from those of the human variety: Above Lestrade's chair, on a makeshift perch, sat Bandu the parrot.

"Come in, Watson!" he chirped in his strange, unearthly voice.

Holmes smiled. "You see, Watson—that bird really does like you."

"What's he doing here?" I said, surprised to see poor Wiggins' pet in the offices of Scotland Yard.

Lestrade rose from his chair. "The bird is temporarily in custody." He coughed and glanced at Holmes. "I, uh, thought it might have some information still to impart," he said gruffly, his face reddening. "I understand the bird was useful to you in discovering who killed Mr. Wiggins," he said to me.

"Quite right," said Holmes, gracefully ignoring Lestrade's

embarrassment. If ever a man understood the desire not to appear soft-hearted, it was Holmes.

"So there's still no sign of Freddie Stockton?" said Holmes.

"No, but I have a few lads out looking for Mr. Stockton as we speak," Lestrade replied. "I fancy it won't be too long before he is brought to justice."

"Did Holmes tell you about–" I began, but Holmes cut me off.

"I was just getting to that, Watson," he said, giving me a significant look. I nodded and sat in the wooden captain's chair across from Lestrade's desk.

"–getting to that, Watson," said Bandu, bobbing up and down on his perch. Lestrade glanced at the bird with an annoyed expression and then turned back to us.

"Yes, what was it you were about to tell me when Dr. Watson entered?"

But just then we were interrupted by a knock on the door. "Yes?" said Lestrade.

The door opened and a stocky young sergeant entered. He had close-cropped blond hair and a military bearing, and when he saw Lestrade he saluted smartly.

"Yes, Morgan; what is it?" said Lestrade.

"Begging pardon, sir, but there is something I think you should know."

"Well, *out* with it, man; what is it?" Lestrade said impatiently.

Morgan hesitated, glancing at Holmes and myself.

"It's all right, Morgan; these gentlemen are helping me with my investigation," said Lestrade wearily.

"Well, sir, it seems that Freddie Stockton has been found–"

"Yes?" Lestrade said, half rising from his chair.

"–floating in the Thames, sir."

"He's *dead*? Are you telling me Stockton is *dead*?"

"Well, yes, sir. I mean, it looks that way, sir."

"Either he's dead or he's not; it's not a question of how he *looks*!" Lestrade bellowed.

"Well, he's definitely dead, sir. We got a mate of his to identify the body—and that hair of his, sir; it's quite unusual. It seems he'd been strangled first, sir, and then the body thrown into the river."

"How could he be *dead*? How can that be?" Lestrade barked, his voice choked with rage.

Startled, Sergeant Morgan took a step backwards. Lestrade sighed deeply.

"Never mind, Sergeant… that will be all, thank you."

Sergeant Morgan saluted smartly, turned on his heel, and left. Lestrade shook his head.

"That Morgan… still thinks he's in the military, what with all that bloody saluting," Lestrade muttered. He rose from his desk and poured himself a glass of water from a pitcher which sat on the windowsill directly behind Bandu. The parrot followed his movements with interest, and when the bird saw the water he opened his mouth and stuck out his odd, sharply pointed black tongue. Lestrade held the glass out to the bird, who drank from it, pointing his face skyward to swallow.

"I think I can explain, Inspector," said Holmes. "You see, when Dr. Watson and myself interviewed Mr. Stockton he expressed some fear of… reprisal… from his employer if he told us anything. At the very least, it was not good for him to be seen with us."

"His employer? And who is his employer?" said Lestrade.

Holmes interlocked his fingers and looked directly at Lestrade.

"There is a man, Inspector, who was behind half of what was evil in London, a man who—"

"Yes, yes," said Lestrade wearily. "I've read Dr. Watson's accounts of the evil Professor Moriarty. Not that I believe a man like that ever existed, mind you," he added with a wink at me. "Still, it makes good fiction, doesn't it?"

"I assure you, Inspector, Professor Moriarty is very real—and not only that, he is very much alive," Holmes replied.

Again Lestrade looked at me, imploringly this time, but I nodded my head.

"I'm afraid Holmes is quite right, Inspector. Moriarty also survived Reichenbach Falls."

Lestrade's face went red. "But—but how... I mean, how is it that I don't know about him?"

Holmes shrugged. "Most people don't know of his existence. That has always been the secret of his power. However, having returned to London to find his empire in a shambles, he is acting more desperately now to reassert his control. His movements have become more open—and more reckless. His challenge to me has an air of bravado about it, something I would never have expected from him in the past." Holmes leaned forward, resting his sharp elbows on his knees. "It is this alone which gives me hope that we may actually overcome him. Before he acted out of a cold self-interest; now he is acting from vanity."

"So he really does exist?" Lestrade said softly, sitting down again.

"I'm afraid so," Holmes replied. "And I am quite certain that he is responsible for Stockton's death. He no doubt wished to make an example of Stockton, who, after all, made not one but two mistakes."

"Two mistakes?" said Lestrade.

"The first one was killing Wiggins," I said.

"You mean Wiggins was not meant to die?"

"Oh, no," said Holmes. "Stockton was just sent to get information out of him, but he died before Stockton got what he came for. He died of strangulation—which was, I believe, how your sergeant said Stockton was killed."

"Moriarty's idea of poetic justice," I said.

"I see," said Lestrade. "And the second mistake?"

"Why, talking to us, of course. We made no secret of the fact that we were looking for Freddie Stockton. During the course of our search, we must have been seen by half the criminal population of London," said Holmes. "He didn't really tell us anything we didn't already know, but he did confirm my suspicion that Moriarty was alive and in London." He then described our interview with the late Freddie Stockton, including our visits to the various places of debauchery. While he talked, Lestrade idly stroked Bandu's feathers, and the parrot responded by rubbing its beak against his shoulder.

"Well," he said when Holmes had finished, "if this is what he does to his own men, he is even worse than I thought."

Holmes smiled grimly. "Oh, he is worse than anyone can possibly imagine, and I hope for your sake that you never come up against him face-to-face, Lestrade."

These words cut Lestrade's vanity, and he bristled. "I am sure I shall be equal to the task, should the time arrive, Mr. Holmes," he said stiffly.

"Of course, of course," Holmes replied genially. "Still, it is a ruthless player who eliminates his own man, and I can't help but wonder what he has in mind next."

"Oh! That reminds me—I have something to show you," I said, fishing around in my pocket for the slip of paper I had shoved in it before I left my office. "Here, what do you make of this?" I said, handing it to Holmes.

He studied it for a moment and then gave it to Lestrade.

"It is simplicity itself; don't you agree, Lestrade?"

Lestrade looked up from the paper. "Why, it's some sort of code, I suppose," he said.

"You are correct there," said Holmes. "It is a chess move."

"A what?" Lestrade studied the paper.

"It's written in the shorthand which chess players use to indicate a move. 'K.Kt.-B4' means that the king's knight—which is of course the knight closer to the king—moves to the square known as Bishop Four; in other words, four squares in front of the bishop."

"Oh, right; of course," Lestrade said, shifting uncomfortably in his chair.

"Where did you get this, Watson?"

"It was in with my mail."

"What was the postmark?"

"There was none, and no return address either... but the man who delivered it matched the description of the strange little fellow who gave me the newspaper in the train station. McKinney said he had muttonchop whiskers; and he came and went without a word."

Holmes' eyes narrowed. "Ah! As there was no message in today's *Telegraph*, I expect that this is his next move, then." He studied the paper. "This could mean so many things; it all depends on proper interpretation."

"I don't understand," said Lestrade. "What do you mean by 'his next move'?"

Holmes proceeded to explain the affair of the missing jewel, stressing that it was a matter of great national importance. Lestrade's eyes widened with each detail, and when Holmes finished he gulped.

"Well, I'll be," he said softly, pouring himself another glass of water from the pitcher behind his desk.

"You see," Holmes continued, "Wiggins' death was one of the moves in... a kind of chess game."

Lestrade received this information with some skepticism but agreed to follow Holmes' lead in the matter.

"That part sounds a bit far-fetched to me," he said a bit sullenly, "but if you think that's what he's up to, I suppose it can't hurt to go along with it…"

"I do, and my brother Mycroft agrees with me," said Holmes.

"Oh, he's in this, too, is he?" said Lestrade. "He's a smart one, is Mr. Mycroft Holmes, but… well, if you don't mind saying so, a bit odd. That club of his…" Lestrade shook his head. "And why is it this Moriarty fellow is tipping you off to what he's up to?"

Holmes leaned forward, resting his arms on the front of Lestrade's desk.

"I believe he feels the need to establish his superiority once again amongst his lieutenants in order to exert the same kind of control he had before he was injured. You see, he has been out of circulation now for over three years, and a lot has changed in London since then. He is playing such a dangerous game to show that he is still the mastermind criminal he once was. But beyond that, there is his arrogance. In fact, his sense of intellectual superiority is the closest thing he has to an Achilles heel. It may be his only weakness, Lestrade, but we must take advantage of it if we are to defeat him."

"What do you think he means by this, then?" said Lestrade, holding up the paper containing the chess move.

Holmes leaned back in his chair. "I'm not certain, but I have several theories. We can't cover all the possibilities, but we must try to do our best. The first thing you could do is to alert all of your men that a move is expected."

"What exactly is… expected?"

"It's difficult to tell. It all depends upon interpreting this move correctly. You have already no doubt given orders to inspect any suspicious ships or other conveyances leaving London."

"Uh, yes; I was just about to do that," Lestrade said. "I'll, uh, tell Morgan to get on it right away." Lestrade went to the door and opened it. "Morgan," he called, "come in here."

A moment later Morgan's ruddy face appeared in the doorway.

"Yes, sir?"

"See that an extra man is posted around all governmental buildings and other places which might be a security risk. And put a couple of extra men at 221 Baker Street, will you?" Lestrade turned to Holmes. "Now that *he* knows you are on the case, so to speak, it can't hurt to have some extra protection."

Holmes nodded. "That's very good of you, if you can spare the men."

"I can. Have you got that, Morgan?"

"Yes, sir." Morgan turned to leave.

"And Morgan—"

"Yes, sir?"

"See that the—the earlier orders regarding the ship inspections are carried out."

Morgan looked puzzled. "What orders, sir?"

Lestrade looked at us and rolled his eyes. "The order I gave you earlier about inspecting all suspicious-looking vehicles leaving London."

"Oh, *those* orders! Yes, sir—right away, sir." The young sergeant saluted smartly and withdrew. Lestrade closed the door and sat down at his desk.

"Morgan will be the death of me," he said.

I looked at him with what I hoped was a sympathetic expression. I couldn't be sure, but I think Holmes was suppressing a smile.

"All right, what next?" Lestrade asked.

"Now we wait," replied Holmes. "Or rather, you wait, as I have a few matters to attend to. Shall we go, Watson?" he said, rising from his chair. Lestrade followed us to the door, a wistful expression on his ferret-like face.

"I'll be in touch," he said. Just then Bandu left his perch and, with a great flapping of wings, settled on Lestrade's shoulder. Lestrade looked both pleased and embarrassed by the bird's behavior.

"Well, Lestrade," said Holmes as we left, "I do believe that bird's taken a fancy to you."

"Oh, that's nonsense," said Lestrade.

"Nonsense," Bandu echoed, "that's nonsense."

Nine

When we returned to Baker Street, Mrs. Hudson met us at the door. I have often described her as long-suffering, which is true, but equally true is that her hardy Scottish nature revels in the constant aura of adventure which surrounds her famous tenant. In short, though she might not admit it, Mrs. Hudson has often displayed a certain exhilaration in her proximity to Holmes—even when the dangers to herself are as real as her recent kidnapping. Now she met us in the hallway, her face animated with unspoken questions.

"There's a young woman upstairs waiting to see you," she said with a conspiratorial nod to me.

"Thank you, Mrs. Hudson," Holmes said, ignoring any implication that he reveal anything more to her. When it came to women— excepting of course the much-admired Irene Adler—Holmes tended to be old-fashioned. Women aroused in him a protective instinct, and he did not relish the idea of exposing them to the perils which his profession occasioned. This attitude was not entirely confined to women; he sometimes expressed a regret that my association with him exposed me to dangers—dangers which I risked gladly but which he felt responsible for.

When we opened the door to the sitting room, Violet Merriweather rose from her chair by the fire to greet us. As she did, the aroma of Golden Nights wafted up from her rustling skirts. The smell of it made me quite dizzy, and I stood there transfixed for a moment.

"Mr. Holmes, I hope you don't mind—" she said, looking flustered. Holmes smiled and closed the door behind him.

"Not at all, Miss Merriweather; I am sorry if we have detained you."

"Oh, I didn't have to wait very long."

"Long enough to smoke two cigarettes and take a nap."

Our visitor blushed, and again I was struck by what an agreeable change it made in her complexion.

"But h-how did you—?" she stammered.

Holmes smiled again and sat in his chair by the fire. As Miss Merriweather was seated in my usual chair, I perched upon the arm of the sofa, the better to hear what Holmes had to say.

"Well, for one thing, I detect the aroma of a blend of Turkish tobacco which, as it happens, neither Watson nor myself use," he said, removing his coat and hanging it on the bentwood coat rack. "As for the nap, I hope you will forgive my impertinence when I observe that the impression upon your cheek was made by the lace doily on the back of that armchair. As I see you are now in a rather agitated state, I presume that only sleep would have induced you to remain in the chair in one position for so long. Am I correct?"

"Indeed you are, Mr. Holmes, and I hope you and Dr. Watson don't think the less of me for my indulgence in such an unladylike habit."

Holmes merely smiled and shook his head; for my part, I had to admit that it only added to our visitor's sense of mystery. What sort of life had she led, I wondered, that she took up such a habit as smoking?

Miss Merriweather herself interrupted my ruminations. "Once again, I am startled at the breathtaking speed of your conclusions, Mr. Holmes."

Holmes shrugged. "Mere child's play. Unfortunately, more important deductions are often harder to come by," he said seriously.

"Is it true, then, Mr. Holmes? Has the Star of India fallen into other hands?"

Holmes lit a cigarette.

"I'm afraid so, Miss Merriweather. It is entirely my fault; I should have foreseen what would happen."

"But Holmes—" I began, unwilling to let Holmes take the blame, but he interrupted me.

"No, Watson," he said. "I am perfectly prepared to accept responsibility for my mistakes. The disappearance of the Star of India is entirely my fault. I am sorry, Miss Merriweather; I have failed you, and now I can only endeavor to right the wrong. I can assure you that if I do retrieve it, it will not easily be wrested from me again. That much I can promise you."

Violet Merriweather looked at Holmes, and though I am by no means an expert on women, I think I know enough to recognize that particular light in a woman's eyes. A slight blush crept into her cheeks, and she cast her eyes down demurely. At that moment I was certain that she had begun to feel something for my friend. I cannot say that I blamed her, although I could well wish myself in his place. With his restless nature and his dedication to reason, Holmes was not of a domestic disposition, whereas I was made for married life. Such things were, at present, out of the question with the lovely Miss Merriweather; the great personage who currently bestowed his favor upon her certainly far eclipsed both Holmes and myself both in renown and resources.

If Holmes noticed Miss Merriweather's emotional response to him, he made no sign of it.

"The important thing now, Miss Merriweather, is that you convey to His Majesty my assurances that I will do everything in my power to maintain the stability of the political situation."

Violet Merriweather grew pale. "Do you mean to say there are political issues at stake?"

"Forgive me, Miss Merriweather; I assumed that you had His Majesty's full confidence, but I see now that you do not have complete knowledge—"

"No, evidently I do not, Mr. Holmes."

"Perhaps he is trying to protect you—"

"Or perhaps he does not trust me."

Holmes looked at me, obviously feeling extremely uncomfortable. I did my best to come to his rescue.

"It is possible that he thought you would be put in a position of some peril if he—"

"—if he was completely honest with me? No, Dr. Watson, I appreciate your attempt to spare my feelings, but if I cannot trust him to be honest with me, then…" her voice trailed off, and I thought she was about to cry. But then she pulled herself up and addressed Holmes in a firm voice. "No doubt you have already surmised this by whatever methods you use to come to your astonishing conclusions, but I am an actress, Mr. Holmes."

Holmes threw his cigarette into the fire and rose from his chair.

"You are correct. I did come to a conclusion early on that you were a practitioner of stagecraft—either an actress or a singer."

"My father was an Italian opera singer; my mother, who was English, was a dancer when she was young. I myself took to the stage at a young age. I mention this now only to show you that I am aware of the enormous social gap which exists between me and—him."

"I see. What *face* was your father's voice?"

"I beg your pardon?"

"What type of voice did he have?"

"Oh, he was… a tenor."

"Ah, so he must have sung the role of Rigoletto."

"Oh, yes, it was one of his favorites." There was a pause, and then she continued. "Mr. Holmes, you refer to a political situation; may I ask what that is?"

Holmes related as much of the current situation as he thought prudent, but it was enough to give Miss Merriweather an idea of what was at stake.

"Then the Star of India never was truly mine," she said. "It was all a mistake, the misguided actions of an impetuous man—"

"—a man who loves you," I felt compelled to say.

She smiled sadly. "Perhaps, but who sees me as little more than an amusing plaything, I fear. I had hoped… well, never mind. How could I suppose that such a great man would continue for long to be interested in me? After all, what can I offer such a man?"

"Oh, a great deal," I said warmly, feeling the blood rush to my cheeks. I looked at Holmes, who regarded me with curiosity. Suddenly, I feared I had revealed too much of my own feelings. But Holmes merely turned to Miss Merriweather.

"Dr. Watson is right," he said graciously. "Never mind the position of the person, it is the trueness of the heart that counts."

Violet Merriweather turned her lovely dark eyes upon him, and I felt certain now that her own heart was beginning to waver. "Oh, do you think so, Mr. Holmes?" she said in a tremulous voice.

"I do, Miss Merriweather, although the world does not always make way for such people. And now, if you will excuse us," he continued, looking at his watch, "Dr. Watson and I have a lead of some importance to follow which concerns this matter."

"Oh, please don't let me detain you," she said, rising abruptly from her chair. "I am sorry if I have taken too much of your time already."

"Not at all," said Holmes, escorting her to the door. "I'll let you know the moment there is anything to report."

"Thank you, Mr. Holmes," she said, taking his hand in hers and holding it a moment longer than necessary.

When she had gone, the intoxicating scent of Golden Nights lingered after her. I now felt quite bewitched by the perfume. I sat there inhaling it as it grew fainter, then I tried my theory out on Holmes.

"She's quite taken with you," I said.

Holmes looked at me as though I were mad. "Nonsense! What on earth gives you that idea?"

"The way she looks at you when you aren't watching."

Holmes snorted. "Good heavens, Watson, next thing I know you'll be writing gossip columns instead of fiction."

"Really, Holmes, she's smitten. You have your area of expertise; allow me mine. I know something more of women than you do, and I say the lady's quite under your spell."

Holmes sat down across from me. "Watson, what you are mistaking for infatuation is merely the hopeful attitude of a young woman who sees in me someone who may be able to help her. What you see as attraction is merely the expression of quite another kind of desire. She may look up to me as someone who can be of assistance—but, really, Watson, I need hardly remind you that her heart is quite engaged elsewhere."

"Very well," I said peevishly. "If you think a woman is incapable of being divided in her affection, you don't know very much about women."

"Did I ever claim to?" Holmes said with a sardonic smile.

I had to admit he had me there. Never has a man made a more public protest than Holmes of his distrust of the opposite sex. Still, I have always suspected he did protest too much, though I never would have said so to his face. He had lost interest in the topic, however, and disappeared into the bedroom only to return with a boxed chess set which he opened and began to lay out upon the sideboard.

"Now we must turn our attention to this information which came to you so mysteriously," he said, studying the note which I had received earlier. "K.Kt.-B4, or king's knight to Bishop Four... let me see. There is already a black knight abroad upon the board–"

"Who is that?"

"Why, the mysterious count who so conveniently jumped over you to capture the jewel."

"Oh."

"So perhaps this is another knight... and if he moves to Bishop Four," Holmes said, turning to a map of London which he had spread out upon the coffee table, "then he should end up approximately here," he said, pointing to the neighborhood of Spitalfields. "Ha!" he cried suddenly, peering at the map. "Of course! Why did I not think of that before?"

"What?"

"Wormwood, Watson, wormwood."

"I don't quite follow you, Holmes."

"Watson, do you recall what lies at the intersection of Bishopsgate and Wormwood Street?"

"No, I can't say that I do."

"Well, I have made it my business to know London as well as other men know their own sitting rooms–"

"Yes, yes, I know! But what lies at the intersection of those streets?" I cried, unable to bear the suspense any longer.

"A pub, Watson, but not just any pub: it is, in fact, the Lancelot Arms."

"The Lancelot Arms? What's that got to do with—?"

"Oh, Watson, don't you *see*? King's knight—Lancelot, in other words—to Bishop Four: The fourth street which intersects with Bishopsgate Road!" He looked at me and smiled.

"How's your East End accent, Watson?"

"Well, I'm not quite the actor you are—"

"Yes, yes—but do you think you can pull it off?" he said impatiently.

I thought for a moment. "Aye s'pose aye can give it a try, what?" I replied, slurring my vowels wretchedly.

Holmes regarded me coldly, as though I were a laboratory animal and he the scientist. "I suppose it will do," he said. "Just let me do most of the talking." He then disappeared into his bedroom and returned with a pile of clothes.

"Here, Watson," he said, tossing some at me. "Do your best to make yourself look disrespectable."

I held up a pair of trousers and a workman's coat, both of which looked as though they had seen better days.

"What are these for?"

"If we are going to be inconspicuous, we must dress as the natives do. Now hurry, Watson; we haven't much time!"

A quarter of an hour later we emerged from the sitting room looking for all the world like a couple of laborers just off work at the docks. A smudge or two of dust and grime on our faces and the transformation was complete. We were about to close the door behind us when Holmes stopped and put his hand on my arm.

"Watson, do you still have your old service revolver?"

"Yes, it's upstairs in my old bedroom."

"You might want to bring it along—and see that it's loaded."

I went upstairs and got the gun from the closet where it had lain unused for quite some time. Apart from my adventures with Holmes,

I had little use for it. I shoved it into my jacket pocket and followed Holmes out the door, still a little mystified by his reasoning.

"I hope you'll be back for supper—I got a nice rack of lamb!" Mrs. Hudson called after us as we hurried out the door.

We quickly hailed a cab. The driver looked at us oddly when we climbed into the hansom—we didn't look like the sort of men who were used to traveling by cab. A thin twilight crept over the cobblestones as we traveled east along Oxford Street.

"You see," said Holmes, "king's knight refers to Lancelot because he was in fact King Arthur's knight… and I thought at the time our little trip to Cornwall was no coincidence. No, I am certain that whatever is going to happen, the Lancelot Arms will figure into it somehow."

Traffic was light and we soon arrived at our destination. The Lancelot Arms had seen better days, but they were far behind it now. The wooden exterior was weatherbeaten and as careworn as an old face, the windows greasy with years of build-up of tallow and the grime from whale-oil lamps. A couple of drunks stood outside the saloon bar, talking loudly.

"Ay say 'e *is*; my brother is certain 'e saw 'im the other night!" one of the men was saying. He was tall and stringy and wore a coat which was several sizes too small for him. His greasy hair fell in lumps about his head, and his teeth had probably never seen the inside of a dentist's office.

"So what if 'e is?" said the other, a little man with a florid face and short stubby hands.

"Nothin'," said the tall stringy one. "It's just strange, that's all. There's somethin' fishy goin' on, that's all."

"Oh, *I* get it, somethin' *fishy*! That's very good, that is—very good indeed," said his companion, laughing. "Fishy, eh? Fishy, is it? Well, that's well done, it really is," he said, slapping his knee as if to wring every bit of amusement he could out of this jest. I personally couldn't make out what they were talking about, but Holmes listened intently.

"Nothing is as it seems in this case, Watson," he said.

I waited patiently for him to explain this cryptic remark, but he did not enlighten me; instead he said, "Mark, Watson, there's more here than meets the eye."

What met the eye inside the Lancelot Arms was a motley collection of working-class fellows: Some of them had the sunburned skin of sailors and dock workers, and others wore the natty red scarves which singled them out as costermongers. They were a rough lot, and I was glad of our disguises, though I worried that we were not as inconspicuous as I would have wished. Holmes, as usual, was unconcerned, and he stepped up to the bar, sliding in between two red-scarved fellows. One of the men—already well in his cups—looked Holmes over and winked at his companion.

"'Ere now, maybe this gentl'man could solve it for us."

Holmes turned to the man. "Solve what?" he said coolly.

The first costermonger smiled broadly, showing teeth yellowed by years of strong tobacco and cheap beer. "Well, guv'ner," he said, exaggerating his accent facetiously, "me an' my mate was wonderin' why is it that there are suddenly so many more coppers wanderin' about certain sections of town, shall we say, than there used to be."

"'At's a right good question," said Holmes. "What're ye drinkin'?"

"Purl," answered the man.

"Oi, barkeep, another round for these fine fellers, an' the same for me an' my friend," said Holmes.

"Much obliged to you, I'm sure," said the costermonger with the yellow teeth. He was taller than his companion, and sported a tattoo of a mermaid on his hairy forearm.

"To yer health," said his friend, lifting his glass to Holmes. He was of medium height and stocky, with a thick neck, a bullet-shaped head, and a dark stubble of beard upon his chin. A worn toothpick hung from his lips, which he never removed, even to drink. I feared he would swallow the toothpick along with the purl, but he was evidently accustomed to his strange habit, and took a long draught of hot purl without disturbing the toothpick.

"Cheers," said Holmes, lifting his glass and drinking. I did the same, though reluctantly. I had never developed a taste for purl, a drink combining hot beer with gin, ginger, and sugar; for one thing, I didn't like gin, which always tasted like medicine to me. But I lifted my glass all the same, following Holmes' lead. I knew he wanted something from these men, though I had no idea what that might be. In spite of the sugar it contained, the drink was bitter, the gin stinging my taste buds with its medicinal aftertaste.

"Care to join us in a game of cribbage?" asked the yellow-toothed man, evidently the leader of the two.

Holmes looked at me. "Wha' do ye say, John, shall we give it a go?"

I tried not to look surprised at his use of my Christian name; I supposed that it was Holmes' attempt to hide our identity. I looked around the bar: through the thick haze of tobacco smoke it was difficult to tell, but I didn't sense that anyone was paying us particular attention.

"I 'aven't played in a while," I said, "but I'm game enough."

"Right," said Mr. Yellow Teeth, producing a pack of soiled, dog-eared playing cards. "I believe there's a table free over there in the corner."

We followed him through the crowded, smoke-filled room over to a round, rough oak table which sat in the far corner of the saloon bar.

"Pull up some chairs for the gentl'men, won't you, Cappy?" he said to his companion, who complied by seizing a chair in each hand and lifting them over his head. I was struck immediately by his strength; the oak chairs were thick and heavy but he handled them as though they were made of paper. I glanced at Holmes, but he was conversing with Yellow Teeth about the terms of the game.

It was said that costermongers did not get up in the morning without a bet placed on the exact hour the cock would crow. Everywhere they went, they gambled. They were a hardworking, hard-driving sort of man, and for a costermonger to play a game of cards without gambling was unthinkable. When Holmes and Yellow Teeth had come to terms over the stakes—high enough to please our host but not so high that he would be enraged if he lost—the game began.

I could tell that Holmes was playing well enough to hold his own, but that he was not trying to win. I followed his lead, and let our companions slowly but surely rack up steady winnings. I didn't know what Holmes' game was, but I was certain that it was not cribbage. I said very little, lest my less-than-perfect accent give me away. However, after several hands and several more rounds of drinks, our hosts had loosened up considerably, and I doubt they would have noticed. Yellow Teeth became downright garrulous, and his stocky companion—whom he continued to address as Cappy—relaxed his muscular neck and let his bullet-shaped head loll back in his chair. Cappy was evidently a man of few words, but in between hands he began to converse with Yellow Teeth in the curious cryptic language of coster mongers, a language I had heard of but which I had never witnessed.

"Skod tienoot," said Yellow Teeth.

"Leereel?" answered Cappy.

"Net Kolko," replied Yellow Teeth.

"Lawcalb?"

"Tire."

During this exchange Holmes was jotting down the score on a piece of paper.

"Well," he said, holding up the paper, "it looks as though you've just about cleaned us out. Yer a couple a good players, you are," he continued, rising from his chair. "And now aye think we'd better be gettin' along now."

"Oh, don't go just yet, guv'ner," said Yellow Teeth, "the cards are bound to turn your way sooner or later... don't you think so, Cappy?" Cappy nodded his assent, chewing on his toothpick.

"Maybe another time," said Holmes, "but my mate and me 'ave to be gettin' on."

"Oh really?" said Yellow Teeth. "Something important, then?"

"Naw," said Holmes, ignoring the fixed stare from Cappy, "but I 'spect someone'd be mad if we didn't show."

"Well, then, per'aps another time, as you say," said Yellow Teeth evenly. "That would be nice, don' ye think, Cappy?"

Cappy nodded and shifted the toothpick to the other side of his mouth. His implacable face made me uneasy, and my hand closed around the revolver in my jacket pocket. Holmes, though, acted totally unconcerned.

"Well, then, thank ye, mates," he said breezily, and I followed him out through groups of dock workers, street hawkers, and ship's mates, all drinking, smoking, laughing, and gambling. Out on the street Holmes turned to me.

"I wasn't sure they'd let us away so easily," he said.

"But you didn't seem worried. Do you mean to say–?"

"Well, it was touch and go for a moment there. Never mind, though, Watson, we've no time to lose!" he said urgently, and set off at a fast pace toward the river.

"Where are we going?" I called after him.

"To the West India Docks!"

The temperature had dropped and a freezing rain had begun to fall, and cabs were hard to come by. We did close to a mile on foot before Holmes finally flagged one down on Cable Street.

"West India Docks as fast as you can," Holmes said to the driver, who turned his horse down onto Aspen Way at a canter. Holmes looked at his watch. "I am afraid Mrs. Hudson will be upset with us; it is far past dinnertime. However, I am far more concerned that we may already be too late for something much more important than dinner."

As we were being jostled about inside the cab, I noticed the burning sensation in my esophagus which was the result of hot gin on an empty stomach. I thought of Mrs. Hudson's rack of lamb with mashed potatoes, and I am ashamed to admit that at that moment I couldn't imagine anything more important than dinner. I decided to try to take my mind off of my stomach.

"Who were those men, and how did you know–?" I began.

Holmes smiled, the pallid light from the streetlamps falling upon his long face. "You remarked of course the red silk neckerchiefs that mark the costermonger as a member of his profession?"

"Yes, of course I noticed that the men wore the red neckerchiefs, but I–"

"Did you also know that they refer to their scarves as king's men?"

"Well, I'll be!" I exclaimed. "So *that's* how you knew they were–"

"–the king's men; in other words, the king's knights. They are more than costermongers, Watson; they are also smugglers."

"Smugglers!"

"Yes. One thing I do know about the Lancelot Arms is that it is a notorious gathering place for smugglers. Our two friends certainly have had some hand in what is about to happen."

"I'll be damned," I muttered. "I don't know, Holmes, sometimes you frighten me." Just then the cab hit a pothole, throwing me to the floor, and I swore.

Holmes reached a hand out to me. "Steady on, Watson," he said, chuckling softly. "I suppose you're also wondering about that curious language they spoke," he continued when I had regained my seat.

"Yes, now that you mention it, what on earth was that?"

"Ah, that was very careless of them. Costermongers often exchange information which they wish to keep secret in a kind of cryptic code which often involves the ability to pronounce words backwards. Do you remember that I was keeping score during the game? Well, I simply copied down what they said—pretending that I was keeping score—and reversed the order of the sounds to find out what they were really saying." He held up the slip of paper which he had used during the scoring of the game. I peered at it and could barely make out the words in the dim light:

"Docks tonight. Really? Ten o'clock. Blackwall? Right."

"That was their biggest mistake," he replied. "They underestimated my ability to crack their code. And really I wouldn't have been able to if I had not been listening for it. Some years ago a case took me to the East End; I learned a lot about the various tradesmen then, and it has always stood me in good stead."

I shook my head in amazement. "Really, Holmes," I said, "I am quite impressed."

"Don't be, Watson, until we see if we accomplish our most important task tonight."

I was dying to ask Holmes why we were rushing toward the river at such a breakneck pace, but now the gin was making me sleepy and I was lulled into a kind of stupor by the swaying motion of the cab. I sat gazing out of the window the rest of the way. When we arrived at our destination Holmes sprang from the cab, paid the driver, and asked the man to wait, slipping him a guinea. The man looked at the coin in his hand and then he laughed.

"I'll wait 'ere all night if need be, guv'ner."

"Right," said Holmes, "come along, Watson."

We set off briskly for the quayside, Holmes in the lead, his worn ulster flapping about him like large brown wings. We followed the wooden walkway down to the dockside, and Holmes looked around. Standing ankle-deep in the mud lining the banks of the Thames, trying to shield a lighted candle from the drizzling rain, was a small girl. She couldn't have been more than eight or nine years old. I recognized her immediately as a mudlark, one of the poor unfortunate scavengers who combed the banks of the river at low tide, poking around looking for anything that they might sell: pieces of coal, copper nails, discarded clothing, bits of rope. It was a hard and cheerless life; most of the mudlarks were either crippled, very old, or very young, the youngest ones often being orphans.

"You there!" Holmes called out to the girl who now stood before us, a startled look on her frozen face. "What's your name?"

"Please, sir, I ain't doing anything wrong, sir. I was just tryin' to pick up a few things to sell, sir," the girl said, trembling.

"There, there," Holmes said in a softer voice, "don't be frightened; we mean you no harm. Here," he said, giving her a handful of guineas, "take that and buy yourself some shoes and a proper coat."

"Oh, *thank* you, sir!" the girl said, staring at the coins in her hand as though she were afraid they might run away. "Thank you ever so much, sir!" she said, beginning to cry.

"Now, now," I said, removing my overcoat and placing it around her thin shoulders, "what did you say your name was?"

"Jenny, sir. Short for Jennifer, but everyone calls me Jenny."

"Jenny—what a pretty name," I said.

"Do you think so, sir?"

"Yes, yes," said Holmes impatiently. "Now tell me, Jenny, have you seen any boats come into the docks tonight since you've been here?"

The girl scrunched up her small face in thought, and then she broke out in a broad smile.

"Yes, sir; an hour or so ago, sir, I heard a foghorn! I remember it because it frightened me and I dropped my candle in the mud. It was ever so difficult lighting it again."

"Do you remember which way it was headed?"

The girl thought again. "I'm not sure, but I think it was headed this way," she said, pointing east.

"Thank you," said Holmes. "There is a cab waiting for us over there," he said, pointing toward the road. "Go get in and warm yourself. Tell the cabby that the tall man with the guineas told you to wait there for him."

"Yes, *sir!*" the girl cried gleefully, and shot off in the direction of the waiting cab. Holmes looked after her, shaking his head.

"It is a heartless society that allows such situations to exist." He sighed and turned back to look in the direction the girl had pointed. "So, they've gone east, have they?" he muttered. "Come along, Watson. We shall see if the trail is still hot."

I followed Holmes along the embankment for a quarter of a mile, past boathouses and wharfs, rotting piers and innumerable small river crafts sitting at their moorings. As we rounded a sharp bend in the river we saw a ship's light in the distance.

"Quickly, Watson, we haven't a moment to lose!" Holmes cried, setting off at a run toward the ship. I followed, coatless, the rain coming heavier now, drenching me right through my jacket to the skin. The ship was a big black freighter, and inscribed on the bow in gold lettering was her name: *Queen of India.*

"The Black Queen," Holmes muttered, and stopped. We could hear voices coming from inside the ship, though we could not make out any of the words being spoken. "I'm going around to the other side," Holmes whispered. "You stay here."

"I'm coming with you," I said firmly.

Holmes looked at me. "They are probably armed."

"I don't care; I'm coming with you. I've got my revolver."

Holmes smiled. "Good old Watson, stalwart to the last."

"I hope not—I mean, I hope this isn't the last."

"I hope so too. Follow me and try not to make any noise."

We walked quietly up to the side of the ship, where she lay tied to her moorings. My hand closed round the gun in my jacket pocket; the feel of cold metal against my palm was reassuring. Suddenly the sound of horses' hooves came clattering across the quay, and Holmes grabbed my arm.

"Quick, Watson, out of sight!" he whispered, and we ducked down behind two mooring posts. From where we were we could see the ship, and we also saw the source of the hoofbeats: An unmarked carriage drove up to the ship, pulled by an enormous black gelding. "Ha—so we are not too late to witness the exchange," Holmes said quietly.

Two men came out of the ship to greet the carriage; one of the men carried a lantern. Two more men descended from inside the carriage; the taller of them carried a wooden box in his hands. Words were exchanged, but again I couldn't make out what they were saying.

"All right, Watson, this is it," said Holmes. "Have you your gun handy?"

"Right here," I said, taking it out of my pocket.

"All right, take off the safety."

"Right."

"Now, I want you to follow me: keep a safe distance, but keep your gun out and pointed at them at all times."

"What are you going to do?"

"Just follow my lead; surprise is of the essence. Quickly, now—go!" And with that, he sprang from behind the mooring post and I followed close behind, my gun drawn.

Our approach was muffled by the falling rain and also covered by a thick fog which had begun to descend, so that the men did not see us coming. Before they knew it we were upon them, and their faces expressed utter astonishment at the sight of us. By now we no doubt looked like drowned rats, appearing out of the harbor mist.

"Good evening, gentlemen," said Holmes in a calm but firm voice. "And now, if you don't mind, I'll take that box," he added, indicating the wooden box. The man holding the box looked at us, his face catching the light from the ship, and I saw with a start that it was Freddie Stockton.

"So, you're not dead after all, Mr. Stockton," said Holmes. "Well, I am relieved."

"Y-y-you're nothing of the s-s-sort," Stockton replied.

"Oh, but I am," replied Holmes. "Though I did begin to suspect as much from a conversation I overheard tonight."

"What?" I whispered.

"The two drunks in front of the pub, Watson."

I remembered their cryptic conversation, and the meaning was suddenly clear to me: They had been talking about Stockton.

"Really, though, Mr. Stockton," Holmes continued, "the thought that Moriarty would dispose of his own man so readily was disquieting."

"If anyone needs disposin' of, it's you," said a snarling voice, and George Simpson stepped out from behind Freddie Stockton.

"Well, you seem to have recovered from our little scuffle the other day rather well," said Holmes genially. "I hope the professor wasn't too dismayed by our little... encounter."

Simpson took a step forward, a look of rage on his ugly face, his little pig's eyes squinting even in the dim light. "I'll take you on any time," he said in a murderous voice.

"Kidnapping women is more your line of work, I should think," said Holmes. "I wouldn't try anything if I were you, or Dr. Watson will be forced to use his gun, and who knows what kind of attention that might attract?"

The two other men, who were dressed as sailors and were evidently crew members from the *Queen of India*, looked at the gun in my hand nervously. They obviously hadn't bargained for anything like this when they agreed to what must have sounded like a simple smuggling arrangement. I held the gun steadily before me, aiming it at Simpson's heart.

"And now, if you would hand over that box, we'll be on our way," Holmes continued.

Stockton hesitated and looked at Simpson for guidance.

"Go ahead," Simpson growled, "'e won't go very far."

Stockton took a step forward and Holmes did the same, holding out his hands. Stockton handed it over to him, all the while keeping his eye on the gun which I kept trained on him during this operation.

"Thank you, gentlemen," said Holmes. "Please give my regards to the professor. Come on, Watson, it's time we were going."

We walked backwards slowly, my gun still trained upon them, until we were swallowed up by the fog and the rain. When we could see them no longer Holmes said, "Now, Watson, run! Run as though your life depended upon it!"

And run I did. I shoved my gun back into my jacket and we tore across the mud-drenched path leading back up toward our waiting cabby, but before we had gone far I heard the sound of gunshots behind us. I began to pull my gun out to fire back but Holmes grabbed my arm.

"Never mind that; it'll only slow us down," he said. "Just run!"

I could see the lights on the side of our cab up ahead through the fog, and I think I never saw a more welcome sight in my life. Just then I heard the sound of another gunshot, and Holmes cried out and stumbled.

"Holmes, are you hit?" I cried.

"It's nothing," he gasped. "I'll be all right. Whatever you do, don't stop! Here," he said, shoving the box into my hands, "take this, in case I don't make it!"

"No," I said, grabbing him around the waist and pulling him along. "We go together or we don't go at all."

He did not argue, but allowed me to half drag him along with me. The cab was just ahead, and the cabby stood waiting anxiously by the door, his whip in his hand.

"What's going on?" he said as we approached. "I thought I heard gunshots!"

"You did," I said, "and if you don't want to get shot yourself, you'll hurry out of here as fast as you can!"

The man evidently believed me, for within seconds Holmes and I were in the cab and we were headed back toward Aspen Way at a gallop. It was only after we were in the hansom for some moments that I noticed a small figure cowering in the corner: Jenny the mudlark.

"Is he going to die?" she said, seeing the blood upon Holmes' chest.

"Not if I can help it," I said, examining the wound. The bullet had grazed his ribcage; it was a nasty gash, though not life-threatening. I was concerned by the amount of bleeding, however, and pressed my scarf to the wound to stem the flow.

"Just lie still," I said to Holmes as he struggled to move. "If you move around you'll only bleed more."

"The box, Watson," he said in an unsteady voice. "Open the box."

I did so, not knowing what to expect, and was astonished to see, nestled in the box's red-velvet lining, the Star of India.

"Good heavens, Holmes, how did you—?"

"I'll explain later," said Holmes, and then he fainted.

As the cab tore through the deserted streets I looked out the back window, but, failing to see any sign of our pursuers, I put down the box and leaned back in the seat, exhausted. Jenny snuggled up to me, whimpering softly, and I put my arm around her thin shoulders.

"Is he dead?" she said in a small voice.

"No, he's just fainted; he'll be all right," I answered in the most soothing tone I could manage. "There, there, now. Why don't you come back with us and we'll give you a nice hot meal and then you can go home to your mother."

"I ain't got a mother."

"Well, to your father, then."

"I ain't got no father either. He went away and then me mother died, an' left only me an' my brother but I don't know where my brother is."

"Good heavens, you mean you're all alone?"

She nodded, and I pulled her closer and stroked her hair as our horse galloped through the night. "Never mind," I said. "You'll be safe with us." But as soon as the words were out of my mouth, I doubted very much that they were true.

Ten

I won't repeat what Mrs. Hudson said when I turned up at Baker Street dripping from head to toe; half carrying Holmes, who was partially conscious and quite weak from the loss of blood; and accompanied by a shivering little waif of a girl—all of us chilled to the bone, tired, and hungry. However, Mrs. Hudson's good Scottish heart melted at the sight of Jenny, and the girl was soon seated in a chair by the fire, wrapped in blankets and sipping hot chocolate.

I laid Holmes upon the divan, removing his shirt and vest in order to examine the wound properly. Mrs. Hudson hovered about, frightened by the amount of blood on his clothes, and even after I assured her that he would be all right she walked around wringing her hands and moaning softly to herself. The bullet had passed between the third and fourth ribs, and although it had not penetrated any organs, there was still the possibility of internal bleeding brought on by trauma. I also detected a fracture of the lower rib, painful but not life-threatening. Holmes was still not fully conscious, and his breathing was shallow.

"Oh, Dr. Watson, what are we going to do?" Mrs. Hudson said, pacing back and forth in front of the fireplace.

"It looks worse than it is, Mrs. Hudson," I said reassuringly.

"Why is he unconscious, then? It frightens me," she said, still wringing her hands.

"He's in shock right now. All we can do apart from dressing his wound is to keep him warm. Now, how about some hot water and a clean towel?"

She scurried off, happier now that she was able to do something. Holmes lay motionless on the divan; I took his pulse and found it weak but steady. I knelt beside him and then was suddenly aware that I was being watched. I looked in the direction of the fireplace: A serious little face peered at me from the depths of Holmes' favorite armchair.

"Yes, Jenny, what is it?" I said.

"Is he going to get better?" she said gravely.

"Yes, he is," I answered. "I wish everyone would stop asking me that."

There was a pause and then Jenny said, "My mum lay down one day and just never got up again."

I looked at her: She clutched the mug of chocolate between her thin white hands as though she would never part with it.

"Jenny," I said slowly, "have you ever had hot chocolate before?"

She shook her head. "I always thought it would taste bitter, like coffee, but it's ever so sweet. It tastes even better than it smells."

I looked at Jenny, wondering how many other things she had never tasted in her short life, but just then Mrs. Hudson returned with a basin of hot water and a pile of towels.

"One towel would have done," I said, taking them from her.

"It never hurts to have too many, I always say," she replied, sitting down next to the couch to watch.

When I began to clean the wound Holmes stirred and groaned.

"Oh, you're hurting him, doctor!" Mrs. Hudson said.

"I'm sorry, but it can't be helped," I said firmly. "I wish you'd just let me do my job, please, Mrs. Hudson."

"Very well, very well; if that's how you feel, I'll make myself scarce. Heavens knows, I don't want to be in the way," she muttered, rising from her chair and scuttling off toward the door. "I mean, I just try to keep a good house and have meals ready on time, and it's not *my* fault if people have to go dashing about in the middle of the night getting shot at and coming home at all hours, drenched to the bone. Come along, dearie," she said to Jenny, "we'll find you a nice soft bed to sleep in downstairs. It's way past bedtime for little girls."

Jenny allowed herself to be led by the hand downstairs, leaving me alone with Holmes. I finished cleaning and dressing his wound and then settled myself in a chair with my pipe to watch over him in case he regained consciousness.

I must have dozed off, because the fire in the grate had burned down to embers when I was suddenly awakened by the sound of Holmes' voice.

"Watson?"

"Yes, Holmes, I'm here." I bent down over him.

"What time is it?"

"I don't know; it's late."

"How long have I been out?"

"Oh, several hours, I should think."

"And the Star of India—where is it?"

In all of the excitement I had quite forgotten about the precious jewel; it still sat upon the mantel where I had carelessly deposited it upon entering the room.

"Don't worry, it's right over there."

Holmes tried to rise up from where he lay on the couch, but I put my hand to his shoulder to stop him.

"No, Holmes, you shouldn't move just yet. I'll bring it over to you if you like."

"Yes, please; I want to see it."

I rose and retrieved the box from where it lay and brought it over to Holmes. He opened the lid and gazed at the stone inside—there it was, unmistakably the Star of India. Satisfied, he lay back down again. I could see, however, that this small effort had exhausted him.

"Very well," he said in a weak voice. "I just wanted to make sure that we have not been fooled."

"What do we do now that we have it?" I said.

"Now that we have it we are in extreme danger," Holmes answered. "Watson, will you do me the kindness of looking out of the window and telling me what you see?"

I did as he asked. "I see two policemen, one across the street and one in front of our building."

Holmes smiled. "Say what you like about Inspector Lestrade, but he is as good as his word. The police presence will help, though it will be no means stop Moriarty from getting at the gem—or at us. No, it would be better if it were hidden somewhere else, somewhere other than here…"

I looked at him: His face was extremely pale and haggard. Beads of sweat glistened upon his forehead.

"Holmes," I said gently, "you must rest. If you do not, I shall insist that you be taken to hospital, where you shall be forced to rest."

"Oh, Watson," he said impatiently, "you said yourself that the injury is not life-threatening."

"No, not if you take care of yourself properly. If you ignore it, however, there is no telling what damage may be done—fever, infection…"

He sighed deeply. "All right, Watson, you have made your point. I will try to rest. Why don't you go up to bed and get some sleep and I promise you I will close my eyes and do the same."

As he spoke I felt a wave of fatigue sweep over me which left me weak-kneed. In my concern over Holmes I had forgotten all about my own exhaustion. "All right," I said, "if you promise."

"I do. Now go to bed."

I dimmed the lamps and went upstairs, fell upon my bed, and was instantly asleep. I awoke to the sound of the streetsweeper's broom, its rough bristles scraping the sidewalk in front of the building. I heard church bells ringing the hour in the distance, and along with the sudden realization that it was ten o'clock, came another awareness: Until this moment I had completely lost track of what day of the week it was. I sprang from the bed, threw on my dressing gown and went downstairs. To my dismay, the couch was empty. I looked in Holmes' bedroom to see if he was there but there was no sign of him. I called for Mrs. Hudson, who appeared at the door holding a coffeepot.

"Mrs. Hudson, did you see Holmes go out?"

"No, Dr. Watson, he must have gone out before I got up."

I groaned. Holmes was in no condition to be running around London at the best of times, much less with Moriarty's men everywhere. I cursed his pig-headed stubbornness and then, not being able to think of anything better to do, I gratefully accepted Mrs. Hudson's offer of breakfast. I was ravenous, having gone without dinner the night before, and put away an amount of eggs and sausages which surprised even me. When I had finished I sat back to smoke my pipe and consider what to do next. It was after eleven and there was still no sign of Holmes, and though I tried not to be, I was worried. As I sat smoking a timid little knock came at the door. I went to the door and opened it: Jenny stood in the hallway in a nightgown much too big for her, her feet clad in oversized woolen stockings.

"Come in, Jenny," I said, and she followed me silently into the sitting room, treading on the hem of her nightgown as it dragged on the floor.

"Where's the other gentleman?" she asked, seeing the empty couch.

"He's gone out," I said.

"Oh." She looked around the room and then, seeing the chess set on the sideboard, pointed to it. "May I play with it, please, sir?"

"Well, it's set up a certain way," I said. "Why don't we see if we can find you something better to play with?"

"Oh, can I just make one move, please, sir?"

"Oh, all right—just one." I walked over with her to the chess set. "Which one would you like to move?" I said, thinking that I would just put the piece back where it was after she had gone. She studied the board, a look of fierce concentration on her little face.

"Have you seen this game before?" I said.

She nodded. "Yes, sir. My brother had one what he found on the street and he used to let me move the little men around the board."

"I see. Did he play by the rules, then?"

Jenny shrugged. "I don't know. I only know that each little man has to move a different way."

"Go on, then, make a move."

To my surprise she picked up the black queen and moved it diagonally so that the white king was in check. She looked up at me. "Now your king is in danger."

I stared at her, and was about to say something, but Mrs. Hudson burst into the room.

"It's Mr. Mycroft Holmes to see you, Dr. Watson," she said, huffing and puffing.

"Thank you, Mrs. Hudson, show him in."

"Come along, dearie," she said to Jenny. "We'd better find some clothes for you to wear."

Mrs. Hudson withdrew, taking Jenny with her, and moments later Mycroft Holmes entered the room.

"Hello, Dr. Watson."

His enormous bulk filled the doorway as he stood there breathing heavily, winded from the unaccustomed exercise of climbing the stairs. I thought about making a suggestion that he get more exercise, but then thought better of it. In some ways he was even more intimidating than his younger brother, with his massive frame and equally impressive intellect. "Good morning," I said.

"Where's Sherlock?" he said, looking around the room.

"I'm afraid he's gone out."

"Hmm. Where has he gone, do you think?"

"I don't know, and I wish I did, because he is in no condition to be out," I said, briefly recounting our adventure of the night before.

"Well," he answered after a moment, "this is disturbing. Do you mind if I sit down?" he said, eyeing Holmes' favorite chair.

"Oh, by all means, please make yourself comfortable. Forgive me—I'm not quite myself today, I'm afraid."

"I understand," Mycroft Holmes replied, settling his bulk into the armchair. "I am quite out of sorts myself. You know how I hate disturbing my routine, and yet I felt compelled to come over here today, only to find that Sherlock is gone."

"Perhaps you can tell me what you came to tell him," I said, sitting across from Mycroft in my usual chair.

"Well—" he began, just as the door opened and Holmes staggered in. He was white as a sheet, and his hand was clutching the wound in his side.

"Holmes!" I cried, leaping to my feet and helping him to the couch. Even Mycroft Holmes looked worried; he rose from his chair and stood over his brother, shaking his head.

"Good heavens, Sherlock, what have you done?" he exclaimed in a voice which, though meant to sound disapproving, could not hide his concern.

Holmes waved his hand weakly. "I'm all right. I just need to rest." He closed his eyes and let his head fall back on the pillow.

"But what on earth—" Mycroft Holmes began, but I held up my hand.

"Forgive me," I said, "but he really should rest undisturbed for a while, if you don't mind."

Mycroft sighed and lumbered back to his chair in front of the fireplace. "Very well, but I have come all this way to tell him—"

"—to tell me what?" Holmes said weakly from the couch.

"Our intelligence sources have just informed us that there is to be an assassination attempt of some kind during Prince Rabarrath's visit later this week. Extremist elements in India consider the relationship between Rabarrath and England threatening to India's independence movement."

"Do you agree?" I asked.

Mycroft shook his head. "No. Rabarrath is a moderate, and is against violence of any kind, either internal or against England. Those who oppose him are the more militant citizens among his own principality, as well as violent factions elsewhere."

"Who... is... in danger?" whispered Holmes. He now sounded so weak that I was about to insist on utter quiet, but Mycroft's next words riveted me to the spot.

"Our sources believe the target of the assassination will be the Prince of Wales."

"*Shah mat*," said Holmes. "The king is dead."

"Precisely. The smuggling operation you fortuitously interrupted yesterday was part of a plan to place the Star of India in the hands of Rabarrath's chief rival in India, Prince Bowdrinth. He is a brutal man opposed to any form of diplomacy between England and India; he also intends to wage warfare against Rabarrath as soon as he feels he has enough of a following. The Star of India could very well be instrumental in giving him that following. It is well that you intercepted it when you did."

"What is Moriarty's game?" I mused.

"Oh, his game is deep, very deep. I doubt that even I understand every facet of it," said Mycroft Holmes. "Where is the jewel, by the way?"

I looked at the place on the mantel where the box had been last night– it was empty. "Good heavens!" I cried, but Holmes' voice stopped me.

"I have hidden it," he said.

"You've *what?*" I could hardly contain my incredulity.

"I've hidden it," he repeated.

"*Where?*"

"In the last place Moriarty would ever think of looking for it."

"Why on earth did you–?" I stammered, but Mycroft Holmes interrupted me.

"Who has been moving these pieces?" he said, pointing to the chess board upon the sideboard.

"Oh, we've had a little girl staying with us, and she was just playing around with it this morning. Here, I'll put it back," I said, moving to the board.

"Don't touch it!" Mycroft's voice froze me where I stood. He walked over to inspect it more closely. "Extraordinary," he said, bending over the board, "quite extraordinary."

"What?" I said, not catching on.

He straightened up and looked at me, his face twisted in a peculiar half smile.

"Well, I don't know quite how to say this, but this little girl has made an amazingly intuitive move."

"She was just playing with it," I said lamely.

"That may very well be," Mycroft answered, "but whatever the reason, she has exactly demonstrated the situation: *She has put the white king in check,* and she has done so using the only piece which could do so in just one move—the black queen!"

"But who *is* the black queen?" I asked, mystified.

"Exactly what I was wondering," replied Mycroft Holmes. "If we knew that, it would all be so much easier."

"Wait! The smuggling ship last night was called *Queen of India.* Holmes even remarked upon it at the time," I offered.

Mycroft shook his massive head. "No, that's only part of the picture. There is another operative here, one I have not yet discerned… Sherlock?" he said, looking over at where his brother lay upon the couch, but Holmes was fast asleep. Mycroft smiled. "I think I'll take your advice and let him rest, Doctor. We're going to need all the help we can get."

Mycroft accepted my offer to stay for lunch, and I must say Mrs. Hudson outdid herself with roast duck and apple stuffing, and I could see that even Mycroft Holmes was impressed.

"Excellent woman, Sherlock's landlady," he said contentedly over cigars and brandy in front of the fire. "She knows how to turn a spit, and yet I have often wondered if it is a lost art."

After sleeping half the afternoon, Holmes awakened long enough to eat something—at my insistence—and now he lay half awake upon the sofa, tossing and turning as Mycroft and I talked.

"Prince Rabarrath is due to come to London on Thursday," Mycroft said, examining the fat cigar he held between his plump fingers. "I actually think my brother did a wise thing in hiding the jewel—assuming of course that he picked a safe place—because if it were returned to His Majesty Prince Edward now, I fear there would be an attempt on his life sooner rather than later. Our sources tell us that the plan is for him to be assassinated during Prince Rabarrath's visit, but my experience informs me that timing in these matters is everything. As my brother said, whoever possesses the jewel now is in great danger. It has become a symbol, and in times of political unrest there is nothing more dangerous than a symbol. I will tell you one thing, though: Your little girl intuited something very important. I've no doubt the black queen is the key to this affair. We must find her or I fear we will fail."

Holmes moaned and I went over to the couch where he lay.

"Holmes, are you all right?"

"Lestrade," he said, "send word to Lestrade the Star is recovered."

"Don't worry, I will; you just rest now," I said, feeling his forehead. It was hot and dry. Just as I had feared, he was coming down with a fever. I pulled the blanket up over him and tiptoed back to his brother.

"How is he?" asked Mycroft.

I shook my head. "His forehead is burning. I am afraid he has a fever."

Mycroft shook his head. "My brother and I should really take a page out of each other's book. He was always too impetuous by half, whereas I... well, as you can see, doctor, I am far too lazy." He sighed. "A happy medium between the two of us— now there you would have a well-balanced, contented man."

I looked at Holmes, turning and moaning in his sleep. Well-balanced, contented... these were not words anyone would use to describe my friend, and yet I felt certain that if he were more balanced or contented then he would not be Sherlock Holmes.

By the time Mycroft left it was early evening. Mrs. Hudson had taken Jenny out to shop for clothes, and they returned with their arms full of packages, laughing and talking noisily in the foyer. Hearing the child's voice downstairs I had a sweet yet sad longing for a child of my own, a pleasure I had been denied throughout my two marriages. I had not felt it such a terrible loss—the loss of my wives eclipsed everything else— but now with the sound of Jenny's quick little footsteps on the stairs, I found myself full of a nostalgia for my own childhood. I waited by the door for Jenny to come in and show me her purchases, and when she entered, followed by Mrs. Hudson clucking over her like a mother hen, I had an agreeable sensation of domesticity which I had not experienced since my Mary died.

Jenny looked such the little lady in her new clothes that I hardly recognized her. A full twenty-four hours of Mrs. Hudson's good cooking had put roses on her cheeks and a glow in her eye.

"There, Dr. Watson," she said shyly, "what do you think of the nice clothes what Mrs. Hudson has got me?"

"Very nice, Jenny," I said. "You look like a proper lady."

She walked over to the couch where Holmes lay in a deep sleep.

"Is he going to be all right?" she said, stroking his forehead.

"Yes, but you must let him rest," I said.

"There, there, child, let's go see what's in the pantry for us," Mrs. Hudson interjected. "Haven't you worked up an appetite with all this dashing about?"

"You mean we are to have another meal?" Jenny said, incredulous at her good fortune. "I never has more than one or two a day at the most."

"Come along, dearie, and we'll fix you a nice cup of tea with some sandwiches and cakes."

Jenny's eyes filled with tears. "You are so very good to me; I only wish my mum were alive to see this. She would be ever so happy, she would."

Mrs. Hudson escorted her out and as I stood looking after them for some time, my own eyes were far from dry. I sighed and sat down by the fire to wait until Holmes awakened. Before long I felt sleep overtake me, and sank gratefully into its soft pull. I was evidently more tired than I thought, because when I awoke dawn was peering through the curtains.

"Good morning, Watson." To my surprise, his voice came not from the couch but from the other side of the room. I rubbed my eyes and saw Holmes bending over the chess set on the sideboard.

"Holmes! You shouldn't be up yet."

"Nonsense. What have we here?" he said, indicating the board. "Did Mycroft do this?"

I explained to him that Jenny had moved the queen and recounted also Mycroft's reaction to it. When I had finished, Holmes nodded and pointed to the black queen.

"He is, of course, quite right: The queen is the key to everything... But who, I wonder, is the black queen?"

"That's exactly what Mycroft said."

"It is the obvious question." Holmes took a deep breath and winced.

"How are you feeling?"

"Oh, not too bad. A bit of soreness around my ribs, but otherwise I'm fit enough."

"I detected a slight fracture when I examined you. I did my best to tape it up, but you really should—"

"Watson, I appreciate your concern, but we have more important matters before us."

Just then there was a knock on the door and a very sleepy-looking Mrs. Hudson entered.

"Begging pardon, but Inspector Lestrade—" she began, but before she could finish, Lestrade himself barged into the room. He was breathing heavily, his face red.

"What's *this* I hear about you *hiding* the Star of India?" he bellowed.

"Inspector Lestrade, how kind of you to drop by," said Holmes. "Please, won't you have a seat?"

"The minute the gem was recovered it was your *duty* to deliver it straight to Scotland Yard!" Lestrade sputtered. "What on earth were you *thinking*?"

Holmes sat gingerly in his favorite chair and regarded Lestrade with an air of condescending affection. I think in spite of everything, he really liked the little inspector, who right now reminded me of a bantam rooster whose feathers have been ruffled.

"My dear Lestrade," said Holmes calmly, "when you have quite finished I will explain everything."

Lestrade abruptly stopped his blustering and looked quite sheepishly at Mrs. Hudson and myself. I think he even blushed a bit. In any event, his face turned a deeper shade of crimson. He marched over to the sofa and sat down.

"All right," he said, "I'll listen to what you have to say, but it had better be good."

"Mrs. Hudson, I'd be willing to bet the inspector has not yet had his morning coffee—or is it tea, Inspector?"

Lestrade looked positively crestfallen. "Um, tea's fine, thank you," he mumbled.

"Tea all round then, please, Mrs. Hudson, if you would be so kind, thank you," said Holmes. Mrs. Hudson rolled her eyes at me and withdrew.

"First of all, the jewel is quite safe, I can assure you of that," Holmes continued, addressing Lestrade. "Second, did it not occur to you that once the Star of India is in the hands of the 'authorities,' so to speak, that Professor Moriarty will have to resort to desperate means in order to acquire it—even if that means killing someone in the royal family?"

"The royal—*what?*" Lestrade stuttered.

"There are rumors of a planned assassination of the Prince of Wales."

"Good Lord," said Lestrade. "What makes you think—"

"I can't go into all the reasons I have for believing it right now, Lestrade, but suffice to say that the danger is very real. You see, if the Star is still at large, so to speak, then Moriarty will have to concentrate a certain portion of his energy and resources on recovering it. In other words, it is a *decoy* while we try to thwart the more dangerous threat: The attempt against the life of the future King of England."

Lestrade sat staring at Holmes for a moment. "I see what you're getting at," he said slowly, "but why couldn't we just *pretend* that we've hidden it?"

"Oh, Moriarty is far too clever to fall for a ruse like that," said Holmes. "He would find out sooner or later. And besides, there is a leak somewhere in Scotland Yard."

Lestrade stared at Holmes as though he had been slapped. When he spoke, his voice was a hoarse whisper.

"What did you say?"

"I said there's a leak somewhere in Scotland Yard."

Lestrade opened his mouth as if to speak, but no words came. At that moment the door opened and Mrs. Hudson entered bearing a tray of tea and hot cross buns.

"I thought you might need a little nourishment," she said, setting the tray down on the coffee table.

"Thank you, Mrs. Hudson," I said, and began to pour tea for everyone. After Mrs. Hudson had gone, Lestrade still didn't say anything for some moments, and the only sound in the room was the rattling of china as I handed the tea round. Finally Lestrade rose from his chair and stared into the fire, which flickered feebly in the grate.

"I suppose you think me quite an idiot, Mr. Holmes," he said quietly.

"I think nothing of the kind," Holmes replied. "I have had years of dealing with Moriarty; he is so clever that he usually hides every trace of his actions, and it is only by paying very close attention to small details that one is able to decipher his movements."

"That's all very well and fine," Lestrade said bitterly, "but a *leak* in Scotland Yard—that's a bit thick, don't you think?" He sounded as though he were accusing Holmes of planting the leak himself.

"Inspector, believe me, I only just figured it out myself; you shouldn't be too hard on yourself."

"And so how did you figure it out, then?" Lestrade said, a challenge in his tone.

"Well, actually, it was Freddie Stockton."

"Oh, you mean the fellow they found in the Thames?"

"Whoever they found in the Thames, Inspector, it wasn't Freddie Stockton. I can assure you he is alive and well."

"What?" Lestrade put down his teacup so abruptly that it rattled.

"Watson saw him too."

Lestrade turned to me, his eyes pleading.

"Yes, I'm afraid it's true. Holmes and I saw him last night," I said.

"But, why—I mean, who—"

"Who exactly *is* lying in the morgue right now? I'm afraid I don't know the answer to that, Inspector, though I have some ideas... how many men do you currently have working undercover?"

Lestrade shrugged. "Oh, I don't know, around fifteen or so, I should think."

"Have any of them been late in reporting in recently?"

Lestrade screwed up his face. "Well, let me think now... hold on a minute—yes, there is one: Hazelton! We haven't heard from him in a couple of days." His face suddenly fell. "Good Lord, you don't think..." he said unsteadily.

"I think it very likely that it was Hazelton fished out of the Thames yesterday. The question is, who managed to get him identified as Freddie Stockton?"

"Well, he does look a bit like Stockton, except that the hair is different."

"I have a hunch, Inspector, that would be borne up by a trip to the morgue. What do you say, Watson; can you be dressed in quarter of an hour?"

"Certainly," I said, setting down my cup. "Though I don't think you should be running around—"

Holmes dismissed me with an impatient snort.

"One of these days, Holmes," I said, "you are going to regret not taking my advice."

Holmes looked at me, his face serious.

"Watson, may I remind you what is at stake here?"

And so it was that twenty minutes later we were on our way to the city morgue with a very subdued Inspector Lestrade, who sat in the cab hardly saying a word. The morgue attendant looked surprised to see us, but led us immediately into the preternaturally clean storage room, every inch of the white walls and floors scrubbed and shining. I inhaled the sharp, rather sickening smell of formaldehyde, so familiar to me from my days as a medical student.

"Ah, here he is: number eighteen," the attendant said, pulling out the white-sheeted body from its bin. The rolling wheels echoed hollowly through the stark whiteness of the room as he slid the metal tray out with its grisly contents. Holmes lifted the sheet to reveal the man's face. The first thing I noticed was the hair: It was the same curious white-blond shade as Freddie Stockton. The water had done some damage to the face, however, and the features were blurred, so that recognition wasn't an easy task. Lestrade, however, sighed grimly.

"That's him, that's Hazelton," he said sadly.

"This is not his natural hair color, of course," said Holmes.

"No, he has brown hair. Why do you suppose it's like this?"

"To make him look more like Freddie Stockton, of course." Holmes turned to the attendant. "The cause of death was strangulation, I believe?"

The attendant nodded. "That's right, sir."

"He may have even been strangled first and then his hair dyed," said Holmes. "Watson, would there be any way to determine the order of those events?"

I shook my head. "Not that I know of. The hair even continues to grow for some time after death, so that some darkness of the roots could exist in either case."

There was a knock on the door and the attendant rose to answer it. He opened it to admit two police officers carrying a body wrapped in canvas, which they deposited on one of the tables.

"What's this all about, Connally?" Lestrade said to one of the men.

"Fellow by the name of William Strater, sir. He's been murdered—an East End job. Looks like it was a pub brawl. Routine matter, I expect, sir."

"May I see?" said Holmes to the attendant.

"Certainly, sir," he answered. He was a small, dapper man with thick glasses, and looked more like an accountant than someone you would expect to find working in a morgue. When he lifted the sheet, Holmes whistled softly.

"Have a look at this, Watson."

I did, and saw at once what had made Holmes whistle: There upon the table, was our cribbage partner from the Lancelot Arms, throat cut from ear to ear, his neck a horrible red grin.

"Good heavens, it's Yellow Teeth!" I exclaimed. Lestrade and Holmes both looked at me curiously. "Oh, I—that's what I called him. I mean, because of his teeth, you see?" I said lamely.

"Do you know this man, Mr. Holmes?" said Lestrade.

"We met him two nights ago at the Lancelot Arms," Holmes replied. "He knew about the attempt to smuggle the Star of India. In fact, it was he who gave us the information, though he was unaware he had divulged the secret."

"So we're not the only ones with information leaks," Lestrade said with some satisfaction.

"That could explain his turning up here!" I exclaimed. "When Moriarty found out the information had been leaked, he had this man killed as an example."

Holmes looked at the body lying on the table. "Yes... I wonder how many more will have to die before this is all over?" he mused. "First Mr. Wiggins, then Hazelton, and now this fellow Strater."

Lestrade sighed and shook his head. "Poor Hazelton... he was about to go on holiday."

"Didn't his wife notice he was missing?" said Holmes.

Lestrade shook his head. "He wasn't married. The ones we use for undercover mostly aren't; it's a difficult job, you know, and often the hours are long..."

Holmes nodded. "I see. They picked their victim carefully. I wonder why Hazelton, though? Was he getting too close to them, perhaps?"

Lestrade shrugged. "I had him working in an opium den—perhaps you know it—the Bar of Gold? It's a meeting place for smugglers."

"Oh, I know it well," said Holmes. "I have on one or two occasions been there myself. On official business, of course," he added, seeing Lestrade's surprised look. "Perhaps it's time to pay another visit," he said thoughtfully. "Maybe I can find out what Hazelton was on to."

"Holmes, do you think it wise?" I said. "I mean, look at what happened to Hazelton."

Holmes smiled. "With all due respect, Watson, Hazelton was neither prepared nor equipped to deal with Professor James Moriarty."

Holmes' tone expressed his usual confidence, but I couldn't help wondering whether anyone was prepared for such a daunting task.

Eleven

At Lestrade's request we returned with him to Scotland Yard. When we entered his office, there, sitting on Lestrade's desk, was a large shiny brass birdcage, tied around with a broad red ribbon. Lestrade looked at us and then at the cage; then, without a word, he went to the door and opened it.

"Morgan!" he called, and the young sergeant appeared at the door.

"Yes, sir?"

"What is this?" Lestrade said, indicating the cage.

"Well, sir, it's a sort of… present."

"A present?"

The young man blushed and stared at his smartly polished shoes. "Yes, sir. You see, sir, me and the lads thought that since you're going to keep the parrot you might like to have a nice cage for him to live in when you're not around. The fellow at the pet shop says parrots like a nice comfy cage. He said it makes them feel secure, like."

"Oh, he did, did he?"

"Yes, sir—do you like it, sir? I picked it out myself."

Lestrade looked at the cage, then at the floor, his face working. I looked away and Holmes coughed delicately.

"It's very nice, thank you," Lestrade said finally, his voice thick.

"I'm glad you like it, sir. I'll tell the lads; they'll be pleased as well." Morgan stood there for a moment and then he pulled himself to attention. "Right... well, then, I'll go back to my desk duty, sir, if that's all."

"Where is he, by the way?" said Lestrade.

"Who? Oh, you mean the parrot? Oh, I've been looking after him, sir, until we found out if you like the cage or not. I'll bring him right round and then he can get acquainted with his new home. We thought it best for you to introduce him to it, sir."

"Yes, that seems the best thing."

"Yes, sir. Thank you, sir."

"Thank you, Morgan."

We followed Lestrade into his office. There was no more mention of parrots or cages, though the handsome brass cage sat behind Lestrade's desk during our entire visit.

"I have some ideas about how to solve your... problem," Holmes said softly. He scribbled something on a piece of paper and slid it across Lestrade's desk. Lestrade read it, his face impassive.

"All right," he said. "I'll await your instructions."

"Right," said Holmes. "Well, I'm off to do my best to impersonate an opium addict."

"Oh, right, the Bar of Gold. Do you want me to post a couple of lads outside the place to keep an eye on you?"

Holmes shook his head. "It would just alert them that something is up. It's best if I go alone."

"All right, then—good luck."

"Thank you, Lestrade. Well, Watson, shall we go?"

* * *

"Who would have thought Lestrade had a soft spot for birds, of all things?" said Holmes as we left the imposing stone turrets of Scotland Yard behind us. "It just goes to show, Watson, that you never know about people."

"No, I suppose not." I thought of Holmes and our long association, and wondered if there were aspects of his personality which would always remain a mystery to me. I looked at him– he was very wan and pale, and I couldn't help noticing that his hand was pressed to his left side as we walked. "Holmes, I think you should rest a bit before you go rushing around again," I said.

He sighed. "Watson, I appreciate your concern, but really, I'll be all right."

If I had known at the time just how wrong he was I never would have let him walk back out the front door of 221B Baker Street.

When we arrived at Baker Street, Mrs. Hudson greeted us at the door.

"Miss Merriweather is waiting upstairs, Mr. Holmes," she said, wiping flour from her apron, her face red from the heat of the kitchen. "I didn't know when you'd return, but I told her she could wait; I hope you don't mind."

"Perfectly all right, Mrs. Hudson," said Holmes, and we went upstairs to see our visitor. The curtains were drawn; a filmy light filtered in through the windows, falling on the graceful head and shoulders of our guest, resting gently on her smooth black hair. She sat looking out the window, and turned toward us as we entered.

"Oh, Mr. Holmes, I hope you don't mind my waiting for you," said Violet Merriweather, rising from her chair by the window. With the light behind her I couldn't see her face; she stood there wrapped in a misty yellow glow. Again I felt the heady fragrance of Golden Nights.

Instead of bothering me, the scent now intoxicated me, and I stood there for a moment drinking it in.

"Not at all, Miss Merriweather," Holmes replied. "It has become something of a pattern. If you would inform me in advance by telegram that you are coming, you would not be inconvenienced by having to wait."

Miss Merriweather took a step toward us and lowered her lovely dark eyes. "Oh, I don't mind," she said, "and I really don't have anything in particular to ask of you..." her voice trailed off and she regarded Holmes shyly from under her thick black lashes. However, if Holmes was aware of the import of her gaze, he made no sign of it. He plucked some tobacco from the Persian slipper which hung over the fireplace, and sat down to fill his old clay pipe.

"Please sit down," he said to Miss Merriweather without looking at her, as though he were entirely absorbed in filling his pipe.

"Thank you," said she uncertainly, and sat upon the sofa.

"Would you care for some tea?" I said lamely, to fill the empty air.

"Oh, no, thank you—Mrs. Hudson has been plying me with all sorts of delicacies in your absence. She said she didn't know where you had gone."

"We just came from Scotland Yard," I said.

"And is there any news?"

I was about to say that the Star of India was quite safe, but Holmes spoke first.

"I'm afraid not," he said, "though I believe a parrot of our acquaintance has found a good home there."

"A parrot?" she said.

"Oh, yes; the chief inspector there has taken a fancy to him, it seems. Do you think he'll keep the parrot's name, Watson? Oh, what is it? It's really very clever; it's an Indian word meaning 'friend'."

"Oh, yes," I said, "it's—"

"*Dost?*" said Miss Merriweather helpfully.

Holmes looked at her. "No, that's not right—wait! I have it: it was Bandu. Actually, now that I think of it, I believe our late friend Wiggins told us that it's a Bengali word."

"Oh, of course," she said, smiling. "*Dost* is a Hindu word."

"You speak the language, Miss Merriweather?"

"Well, I spent some time there as a child. My parents toured quite a bit, and my brother and I were always—"

"Oh, you have a brother?" said Holmes.

"I had a brother, Mr. Holmes. He was killed in an accident when we were children."

"I see; I am very sorry."

I for one did not see how Holmes could be failed to be moved by this lovely creature sitting before us, whose life was such a strange combination of tragedy and drama, but he seemed as indifferent as ever, and sat puffing placidly on his pipe.

"Well, I am sorry to have taken up your valuable time," said Miss Merriweather, rising from the couch and moving toward the door. "It is just that I am so concerned about—well, you understand, Mr. Holmes. I have been given to believe that much is at stake in this affair."

"Oh, you are quite right, Miss Merriweather," Holmes said. "There is much at stake indeed, perhaps more than even you know."

She looked at him curiously and then slid her arm into the sleeve of the coat which I held for her. "If any man can unravel this Gordian knot, I am sure you can, Mr. Holmes," she said.

"I shall do my best, I can assure you," said Holmes.

I escorted Miss Merriweather to the door.

"Thank you for your kindness, Dr. Watson," she said.

"Not at all, Miss Merriweather," I said, opening the door for her.

"Good-bye, Mr. Holmes."

"Good-bye," Holmes called out over his shoulder, his mind already somewhere else.

"Good-bye," I said, and closed the door after her. A lingering scent of Golden Nights trailed after her. The combination of the perfume and the lack of sleep made me feel quite giddy, and for an instant I thought I might pass out.

"Steady on, Watson," said Holmes without looking at me.

I walked unsteadily over to my chair and sat down across from Holmes. He sat smoking his pipe, an impenetrable expression on his leonine face.

"Holmes," I said, "I do believe you don't trust Miss Merriweather."

He shrugged. "She is a woman, Watson, and trusting them has always been your department. As for me—well, you know my views on the subject."

"But, Holmes, can't you see that she is quite infatuated with you? She likes you; take my word for it."

Holmes looked at me. "Does she?" he said softly. "I wonder."

After much effort, I persuaded Holmes to rest that night and visit the Bar of Gold the following day. We dined at Baker Street. At precisely seven o'clock Jenny came into the room, curtsied, and informed us that dinner was ready. Mrs. Hudson had by now entirely taken Jenny under her wing. The frightened, haunted look on the girl's face was beginning to fade, and her eyes were alive with the healthy curiosity of a normal child.

After dinner I persuaded Holmes to go up to bed, and I myself followed soon after, feeling quite exhausted from the events of the past few days. I dreamed of Miss Violet Merriweather: In my dream we walked together hand in hand through the streets of London, she dressed all in white. As we walked the skies darkened and a torrential rain began to fall. We ran for cover, but as we ran the cobblestones began to transform under our feet–to my horror, they turned into the squares on a chessboard. I looked at Violet–her white dress had become soiled with mud and her hand was suddenly torn from mine–and then I awoke. I sat up in bed, and as I did I smelled the unmistakable aroma of shag tobacco. I put on my robe and crept downstairs.

I found Holmes sitting in front of a cold fire; the flame had long since burned down to glowing ashes.

"Holmes?" I said softly.

For a moment he did not respond, and I thought he hadn't heard me. Then he sighed, a long, slow exhale of breath like the whispering of wind in the eaves.

"I couldn't sleep, Watson," he said without looking at me. "I have had the same nightmare several nights running now, and I..." his voice trailed off and he stared into the fire.

"What is it? The nightmare, I mean?" I said.

"I am at Reichenbach Falls again, locked in combat with Moriarty at the top of the precipice. I am trying to find a firm foothold on the rocks, but they are slippery from the spray of the water, and I can feel my feet sliding out from under me... I struggle to regain my balance, but I can't. I feel Moriarty begin to go over the edge but I cannot loosen his grip on me, and I fall with him. We fall for what seems like eternity, down, down into the swirling vale of water... and then I wake up."

"It isn't uncommon to relive traumatic past events in one's dreams," I said. "In fact, there is a man in Germany–his name is Freud, I believe– who has written some interesting things about the way the mind–"

"Yes, yes; I am familiar with Freud's work," said Holmes impatiently. "I'm sorry, Watson," he said, sighing again. "I didn't mean to be rude; it's just that... I suppose I am somewhat rattled by all of this."

"I can understand why," I said sympathetically. "After all, the stakes are enormous, and you—well, you're probably the only man in London who can defeat Moriarty."

"Can I? I wonder… do you know how I said earlier that in order to defeat him I must learn to think like him?"

"Yes, I remember."

"Well, I have done my best to peer into the abyss which is Moriarty's soul, and I find that the line between is a thin one… thinner than I had ever let myself imagine. I suppose instinctively I feared that in that way lies madness…"

I did not reply, but sat down opposite him.

"Consider, Watson: What causes him to use his enormous talents for evil, whilst I turn mine toward the service of my fellow man?"

"I don't know, Holmes."

"I didn't either, Watson, and that's when I decided that in order to defeat him I must *know* him. I look into my own soul and I see nothing but an accumulation of habits: I eat, I smoke, I dabble in chemistry and crime-solving, but really, beyond that, what am I? Surely a man must be more than that, more than a collection of… of routines!"

"Holmes," I said, fearing where this discourse might lead.

"Oh, I know, Watson—you think me terribly moody to brood so on the nature of existence while most people are glad just to be alive. Well, locking horns with Moriarty as I have done these past few days has led me to consider the nature of what we call good and evil."

"And what conclusions have you reached?"

"None whatsoever, Watson; that's the damnable part of it. I'm not sure there *are* any to be reached. I only know that without much difficulty I can see myself in Moriarty's place…"

I wanted to say something, but I could think of nothing.

"When Flaubert was asked how he could write from the point of view of a woman so successfully, his reply was '*Madame Bovary, c'est moi.*'

You see, his genius allowed him to insinuate himself into the mind of a bored, sexually frustrated, middle-class Parisian housewife—and thus he was able to produce his masterpiece."

"And?"

"Well, Watson, in order to defeat Moriarty I must in a sense *become* him, to think as he thinks, to feel as he feels. In other words, I must learn to identify with him, just as Flaubert did with Madame Bovary."

"I see. And have you?"

"I have. It would be wrong to say that I sympathize with him, exactly, but I can say that I have seen what it is that drives him."

"And what do you see?"

Holmes stared into the empty grate, his eyes hooded. "Pain, Watson— horrible, searing pain, which eats at him just as surely as he preys upon society." Holmes rose from his chair and poked at the dying embers. "Where the pain comes from I do not know. I have long considered Moriarty the most perfect reasoning machine I have ever known— except for my brother Mycroft—but now I see a much more complicated picture. I understand now what really drives Moriarty, and, as I said before, we are not so different as all that."

Holmes rubbed his forehead wearily. I looked at him and considered what deep, buried pain might be driving my friend. It was not the first time the thought had occurred to me, but I had never before thought to compare him to Moriarty.

"I have come to the conclusion that there is a single need underlying all of his greed, his villainy, his scheming and plotting," said Holmes.

"And what is that?"

"The need for control, Watson: He must have control of the others around him. He has a vast and unquenchable desire to be in complete control of everything he touches—and that, Watson, is what passes for evil in our society."

"But surely it is—"

"Oh, yes, in his case it most assuredly is manifested in evil deeds; of that there can be no doubt. But in my case, Watson…" His voice trailed off and again he stared into the flickering embers. I shifted uncomfortably in my chair. My relationship with Holmes had always been based upon an unspoken agreement on my part not to pry too deeply into his emotional life. Indeed, the facade he presented to the world was of a man who had no use for his emotions. And yet here he was, revealing parts of himself I would never have dared to ask about. I too stared into the fire and waited for him to resume speaking.

"Watson, do you ever ask yourself why you behave the way you do?" he said finally.

"Well, I suppose that depends on what it is I've done."

Holmes allowed himself a short, brisk laugh. He put some more wood on the fire and sat down again. "Yes, of course. What I mean is the overall patterns in your life. Do you ever examine them—analyze them, as it were?"

I thought for a moment. "I suppose I do from time to time, when I'm not too busy…"

"Interesting you should say that. I've been thinking about my aversion to inactivity… an aversion so strong that I resort to using drugs to counteract it."

"Yes?" I said, holding my breath. Holmes looked at me, his gray eyes glowing yellow in the fire light.

"I'm afraid to come face-to-face with myself, Watson. That is what I use drugs to escape—and that is the same thing Moriarty uses crime to escape."

"Do you think so?"

"I am certain of it. As I said, I have come to realize that I know what he feels: another problem to solve, another adventure to embark upon, and suddenly one is taken out of one's self—and the relief, Watson… the relief can hardly be described." He let his head fall onto the back of the chair, the line of his jaw as sharp as the division between earth and sky.

"I see," I said.

"Do you? I wonder… you see, Watson, one of the conclusions I have reached tonight is that I am in fact more like Moriarty than I am like yourself."

"Oh, Holmes, surely you don't—" I began, but he cut me off.

"Wait, wait; let me finish. What I mean is that you are a good fellow, you have always been a good fellow, and you will always be one, whereas I…" His brow darkened and his tone became ominous. "You see, Watson, I think I could have easily followed Moriarty's path. We are, after all, so much alike: obsessed, driven, uncomfortable men, not at home in our own skins nor among our fellow creatures. We are far too sensitive to the insults of the world, to the dark side of human nature, whereas you—well, you always see the best in other people."

"Holmes, you make me sound positively dull."

"Oh, no, you are not dull; far from it. In your own way, Watson, you are far wiser than I shall ever be, because you have the gift of knowing how to be happy."

"Well, I don't know about that."

"Oh, I don't mean that you are happy all the time, only that you have the instinct and the drive for it—you are equipped for it, you might say, whereas Moriarty and myself… well, I suppose the closest I ever come is during the rare moments when I lose myself in a piece of music, or am so deeply embedded in a case that I cease to think about myself… that passes for happiness, at any rate."

There was a silence and I could hear the crackle of the logs in the fireplace. The tart smell of burning pine mingled with the aroma of Holmes' Turkish tobacco.

"Holmes, I don't know what to say," I said after a minute. "I shall always regard you as the best and wisest of men."

Holmes smiled. "You really should try to avoid quoting yourself, Watson—it gives the impression you've run dry of ideas."

I laughed. "I didn't think you read my stories."

"Oh, I *read* them, I just don't always agree with them."

We both laughed.

"I'm just tweaking you, of course. I appreciate your literary gifts, even though my own interest lean more toward fact than fiction."

There was another silence, this time the comfortable silence which exists between two intimate friends. It struck me that whatever else Holmes and I were to each other, we were also two men who know that come what may, the other will always be there.

"Well," said Holmes after a while, "I think I will go up to bed now."

"I'll do the same," I said.

Holmes rose, stretched his long frame, and yawned. "I rather think I shall sleep soundly now," he said. "Good night, Watson."

It was some time before I did actually go up to bed, however. I had some thinking of my own to do. I put some more wood on the fire and sat staring at the flames for some time. I had always admired my friend, but now I felt an emotion I had never felt before—not quite pity, but something akin to it. I was not sure I liked the feeling, but I had no choice in the matter: By opening himself up to me, Holmes had redefined our relationship. There is within every man a secret soul, a self which he hides from the world's prying eyes, and it is this which he protects as a mother might protect a child. Holmes had always guarded his even more tightly than most men, but now he had given me a glimpse into Holmes the man, with all his vulnerabilities. For my part, I felt a new responsibility to protect him as best I could.

I sat for some time staring out the window as a yellow fog slid along the street and wrapped itself around the lampposts. Somewhere, out in that gathering fog, Moriarty waited.

Twelve

The next morning nothing was said of the conversation from the night before. Holmes was still determined to visit the Bar of Gold opium den and retired to his bedroom immediately after breakfast to dress for the occasion.

I have in the past remarked that the stage lost a fine actor when Holmes decided to become a professional consulting detective, but I have never been more sure of it than that day. An hour or so after lunch Holmes emerged from his bedroom. He was all but unrecognizable: His skin was a papery yellow, and his hair somehow looked thinner and disheveled beyond imagining. His cheeks were even more sunken than usual, and his eyes shone out of hollow sockets with the fevered gaze of the opium addict.

"Good heavens, Holmes!" I said when I saw him. "I doubt your own mother would recognize you—*I* certainly wouldn't, if I saw you on the street!"

"That is just as well, Watson," he said. "Where I am going, I must rely on not being recognized, for if I am..." his voice trailed off, and I shuddered.

"Do you really think this wise, Holmes? I mean, surely there are other ways…"

"There are no quicker ways, Watson! Do I need to remind you that we only have two days now before the appointed visit? No, I see no other way at present," he muttered, adjusting the filthy rags which covered his back. The movement caused him to wince and clutch his side.

"Holmes," I said, but he waved me off.

"Look after things for me, Watson," he said. "This investigation may take some time, but you should hear from me shortly."

And with that, he was gone.

I did not hear from him, not that day or the next. I became very worried, and on the morning of the third day I contacted Lestrade, who sent an agent to the Bar of Gold to try to find Holmes. The agent returned unharmed but with nothing to report, and even Mycroft Holmes was at a loss to explain what might have happened to his brother. I was on the verge of going to the Bar of Gold myself to find out what had happened, but Mycroft urged me to wait, in case I should spoil some plan which his brother had set in motion.

"Prince Rabarrath arrives in London today, and there is to be a ceremony at the Tower tonight to welcome him," said Mycroft as we sat in the Visitors' Room at the Diogenes Club. "I advised against it, considering the circumstances, but the Prince of Wales was adamant that the ceremony would take place. It is certainly ill-advised, and I fear that even with increased police presence something dreadful will happen."

I had the feeling all during our conversation that Holmes was privy to information which I did not have, which wounded my pride; but it was a small matter compared to the fear I felt for Holmes' safety.

As for me, I had nothing better to do than worry. I had given my practice over to my colleague Dr. McKinney indefinitely and I was now more or less living at Baker Street, in hopes of hearing something from Holmes. Mrs. Hudson and I had taken to eating our meals together—because we both missed him, I suppose, and we took some comfort in each other's company. Jenny had become a fixture at Baker Street. Both Mrs. Hudson and I were loath to part with her, and neither of us could bear the thought of sending her to an orphanage.

Monday was All Hallow's Eve, and that afternoon the three of us sat glumly before the fire eating a late lunch. Anyone observing us would have thought we made a strange little family grouping.

"Do you think he's…" Mrs. Hudson said as we finished the last of the mutton chops.

"Still alive?" I said.

She shuddered. "Oh, don't say that, please! No, I was going to ask if you thought he was all right."

I shook my head. "I don't know, Mrs. Hudson. I'm as worried as you are, but there's no telling… I can't say for certain. All I know is that if ever there was a man who could take care of himself, it is Sherlock Holmes."

"Aye, mostly that's true," she said, "but the evil one he's dealing with now… Mr. Holmes has said he's a match for himself."

I nodded. "I know, I know; but all I can hope is that there's a reason Moriarty would not want to kill Holmes outright. I can't help but think that if he had wanted to, he would have done it before this."

Jenny had finished her lunch and sat quietly by the fire playing with one of the dolls Mrs. Hudson had given her. She looked up from where she sat. "Is he going to die like me mum did?" she said.

"No, dearie, he's not going to die," said Mrs. Hudson, and then she addressed me in a low voice. "Is Scotland Yard doing everything they can?"

"I was thinking of going over and talking to Inspector Lestrade about it again," I replied, looking outside. It was a blustery day, but dry enough—although in London there was a saying that it was always either raining, about to rain, just finished raining, or thinking about raining. I sighed. "Thank you for that excellent meal, Mrs. Hudson," I said, rising and putting on my coat.

Mrs. Hudson rose and began clearing the table. "I'm glad you liked it. I wasn't able to taste a single bite myself, I'm so worried about Mr. Holmes."

I noticed that even if this were true she had certainly done justice to her cooking by eating at least as much as I had.

I stood by the door, holding it open. "Well, I'm off to Scotland Yard."

"Good luck, Dr. Watson. I hope you find out something. Wake me up when you come in if there's any news."

"I will. Good night, Mrs. Hudson."

"Good night."

I stood for a moment, looking around the familiar sitting room, thinking how empty it looked without its most dynamic occupant. His pipe lay on the writing desk; the Persian slipper full of shag tobacco sat untouched in the corner. I even missed his untidiness, wishing that he were there to litter the room with his papers, clippings, and files as he had on so many evenings while we sat together by the fire. I sighed and closed the door behind me. As I descended the stairs to the ground floor, I realized that I was also feeling another kind of fear: fear for my own safety. I was going out alone and unarmed, with Moriarty's agents everywhere. If they had Holmes, why not take me too? I thought about taking along my service revolver, but my anxiety to find out about the fate of my friend was greater than my fear for myself. I hailed the first cab and told the driver to take me to Scotland Yard.

I needn't have hurried, for as soon as I saw Lestrade's haggard face I knew there was no news. Lestrade was standing at his desk talking to Sergeant Morgan, and when he saw me he nodded wearily.

"Hello, Doctor—I'm sorry to say we have no leads at all at the present time. He's covered his tracks well, this time—Moriarty, I mean." Lestrade paused and scratched his head. "Oh, that's all; you can go now, Morgan," he said to the sergeant, who had been standing expectantly awaiting further instructions. The man saluted and went off, saluting me as he went by. Lestrade looked after him and shook his head.

"Morgan! Can't seem to break him of the habit of saluting all the time. It gets kind of annoying, I can tell you…" Lestrade sat down heavily, and I could see by the slump of his shoulders and the heaviness in his eyes that he was exhausted.

"Lestrade," I said softly, sitting on the empty chair across from his desk, "why don't you get some rest? You look completely worn out."

Lestrade looked up at me through red-rimmed eyes. "I confess I am a bit done in, Doctor, but…" He ran his fingers through his hair. "I just can't understand why we can't turn up *something,* some piece of evidence, some lead that could tell us where…" He looked at me intently.

"Is it true, Doctor? Is he *really* back?"

I could not prevent the shudder which ran down my back.

"Oh, he's back all right, Lestrade; at least Holmes thinks so. I know it seems hard to believe, but Holmes himself returned from the dead, so to speak, so why not…?" I couldn't bring myself to say his name. Evidently neither could Lestrade.

"Oh, I almost forgot! I suppose you might as well see this," he said, fishing around in his desk. He pulled out a plain piece of paper and handed it to me. On it was written simply: *Check.* I looked up at him. "It came in today's mail—no return address, of course, and no postmark, so it must have been slipped in somehow."

The implication was clear. Moriarty was in the final stages of his game, and had the confidence as well as the audacity to rub our noses in it. I handed the paper back to Lestrade and sat down wearily.

Lestrade looked at me, his face devoid of emotion. "Do you think Holmes is—"

"—still alive?" I finished for him. He nodded grimly.

"I hope so, Lestrade," I said, "I hope to God he is."

When I returned to Baker Street I looked for the two policemen Lestrade had posted to watch the building, but there was no sign of them. Mrs. Hudson had gone out, and had evidently taken Jenny with her. I trudged up the steps wearily, and then stopped when I got to the door to Holmes' apartment. Something was wrong: the door was ajar, and Mrs. Hudson never would have left it that way. It wasn't just that, though; something was different—a smell, a feeling, a presence that I had never felt before, and it raised the hackles on my neck. It was like a palpable darkness, a physical presence of terror. I pushed the door open slowly and entered the sitting room.

I had often heard Holmes describe Professor James Moriarty, but I had never thought that I would meet the man face-to-face. In any event, I was unprepared for the hideous grim scarecrow of a man who sat before me. He sat in front of the fire, silhouetted in the dying embers, his head wreathed in tobacco smoke, and for an instant I had an impression that I was meeting the Devil himself, surrounded by the fires of hell. Moriarty stood up, and I took an involuntary step backwards. His tall form was stooped and on his long white face was an ugly, jagged gash which, though healed, still looked raw and angry even in the dim firelight. He took a step toward me, and I could see that he walked with a pronounced limp.

"Good evening, Dr. Watson," he said in a tone which was all the more sinister for its politeness.

"What are you doing here?" I said in a strained voice which was scarcely more than a whisper.

He laughed, and I will never forget that sound as long as I live. It was the most mirthless laugh I have ever heard: the expression of a deep and gnawing pain, the cry of a tormented soul writhing in eternal anguish. I was chilled to the bone and yet I stood my ground.

"What have you done with Holmes?" I said, my legs trembling under me. I regretted not having picked up my revolver after all, although I wasn't sure what good it would have done me now. His very presence had a way of dismissing all notion of self-defense; he was mesmerizing, like a snake hypnotizing its prey. Indeed, his head actually swayed back and forth slowly as he talked, and the oscillation struck me as distinctly reptilian.

"Well, now, Doctor, I was just about to ask you if you would like to have him back."

"Where is he? What have you done with him?" I said, taking a step into the room. Moriarty took this as a cue to sit again, which he did with a stiffness which I assumed was also a result of injuries sustained in the fall at Reichenbach. He lit a new cigarette.

"Oh, don't worry, Doctor. He is unharmed... well, relatively unharmed, at any rate. I couldn't quite control the vengeful urges of George Simpson. Let's just say that Mr. Holmes is alive and likely to remain that way at least for the time being."

I had an urge to grab him and wring the life from that hideous thin neck, but the thought of touching him produced a feeling of physical revulsion which was akin to nausea. In any event, I assumed Moriarty was armed, and even if he wasn't, killing him at this point would solve nothing, and might even lead to Holmes' death. Without Moriarty to give orders, I was certain that the criminals in his employment would gladly finish off Holmes. I inched toward the window, hoping to perhaps signal somehow to the policemen who should have been standing guard outside.

"Oh, if you are looking for your inspector's men, I can assure you they are unharmed but safely out of the way for the time being. I didn't want any distraction to interrupt our little chat."

"What do you want?" I said, all the fight gone out of me.

"Oh, don't worry; it isn't much," he said, smiling. A smile on that face was hideous. The scar on his left cheek pulled the mouth up more on that side, so that what I saw was the lopsided grin of a demon, as devoid of humor as his hollow laughter. "Just tell me where the Star of India is," he said in a low, raspy snarl.

"The Star of India?" I said, trying frantically to think.

Moriarty lit a cigarette.

"Oh, come now, don't play coy with me, Dr. Watson. It's been a good game, but it's winding down and my patience isn't endless. I know that Holmes knows where it is, and that he told you. I could of course try to wring it out of him, but he is not a man who is persuadable through the use of physical pain." Moriarty shook his head, blowing smoke out of his thin, curved nostrils. "Of course, my boys would have liked to force it out of him, but they are inclined to be a little… rough, shall we say, and I intend to keep Mr. Holmes alive–for the present, at any rate."

At that moment I would have gladly given the Crown jewels themselves in exchange for Holmes' life. I decided to try a bluff.

"All right," I said, trying to stop my voice from shaking. "I may know where the Star is, but how do I know you'll release Holmes if I tell you?"

Moriarty looked at me through a haze of smoke. "You don't," he said. "You will just have to trust me."

"All right," I said, "I will tell you where the Star is, but if you don't release Holmes I swear I'll hunt you to the ends of the earth–"

Moriarty threw back his head and laughed his horrible empty laugh. "Oh, very good, Doctor! Spoken like a true hero of a melodrama. I can assure you this is no play, however," he said, his voice hard, "and that if you lie to me you shall regret it."

"All right," I said, trying to think fast. It was no use, though; anything I told him would be a lie. I sat staring at him, unable to move or speak, my mind sinking into misery as I thought of Holmes and what Moriarty would do to him.

"Never mind," Moriarty snarled impatiently, and moving to the window, he signaled to someone outside. Moments later Freddie Stockton appeared at the door to our sitting room. His white-blond hair glimmered in the firelight, and his little eyes were narrowed cruelly.

"Dr. Watson will be accompanying us upon our return, Freddie," Moriarty said with a languid wave of his hand. "See that you make him comfortable, will you?"

Stockton grinned and advanced toward me. I turned to face him. He made a feint to his left—and too late I saw the bludgeon in his raised right hand. I tried to recover in time to fend off the blow, but I was caught off balance. I felt a crushing blow to the back of my neck, and then everything went black.

Thirteen

I awoke in another kind of blackness, this one relieved only by the faint glow of a solitary streetlamp shining through a single window. As my eyes became accustomed to the darkness I saw that I was not alone. Across the narrow basement room a figure lay upon a mattress on the floor. I tried to move and found that I was tied to the bed I was lying upon, my hands and feet bound securely by rope. The figure across the room lay perfectly still, and I wondered if he were alive or dead. A horrible realization suddenly came over me, and I whispered into the darkness.

"Holmes," I said softly. The figure did not stir. "Holmes!" I said louder. "Holmes, it's Watson." There was a pause during which the pounding in my head drowned out all other sounds, and then the figure moved and groaned. "Holmes!" I said. "Wake up, Holmes!"

It was Holmes all right, and I thanked God he was alive, but I shall never erase from my mind the sight of him on that night. He rolled over so that the light from the window caught his face, and I gasped when I saw it. He was so badly cut and bruised that he was at first almost unrecognizable. It was evident that he had been brutally beaten and was in dire need of medical care.

"Holmes!" I said. "What did they do to you?"

"They—tried to use persuasion on me," he said, and his words were slurred. I wondered if he had been drugged. I struggled to free myself of the bonds which held me, but to no avail; I was bound very securely to the bedpost.

"Holmes!" I whispered into the darkness. "What are they going to do with us?"

"I don't know, Watson," he said weakly. "I confess I'm trying not to think about it."

We were both silent for a while, and I could hear the sound of seagulls outside our window. I also thought I heard the sound of lapping water, and the air smelled of salt and dead fish. The moan of a foghorn cut through the quiet air, and then I was certain: We were being held in a building situated somewhere on the banks of the Thames. Light from the single streetlamp shone in faintly through the window, and I began to make out the outline of our room. It was a narrow basement chamber with walls of exposed brick; the single window was set just above ground level. I craned my neck around so that I could see the landscape outside: It was a bleak view of a deserted dock, with wooden piers jutting out into the water. A solitary seagull sat atop one of the crumbling posts, his head tucked underneath his wing.

"Holmes!" I said. There was a pause, and then he answered.

"Yes, Watson?"

"What are we going to do? We must get out of here!"

"I'm afraid I'm too weak to free myself," he said, his voice faint. "Besides, the window is bolted from the outside."

"We could break the glass."

"We could, but I'm afraid the noise would draw attention to us… what day is it?"

"Monday, All Hallows' Eve."

"Damn! Is Prince Rabarrath—"

"Yes, he's come to London. Mycroft told me that there's to be a ceremony tonight at the Tower of London to welcome him."

Holmes groaned. "We must not let that ceremony take place, Watson."

I didn't see that we were in any position to prevent it, but I said nothing. Holmes must have lost consciousness again, because he lay without speaking for some time. I could hear his labored breathing as I lay there inhaling the damp, musty scent of mildew. Outside I could hear the lapping of the water against the pilings. I heard footsteps, then the door to the room opened and a tall, spare figure stood silhouetted in the door. With the light from the hallway behind him, you could not see his face, but it was unmistakably the gaunt, stooped form of Professor Moriarty. He advanced into the room, and the blood froze in my veins as he bent over Holmes.

"How are we feeling, eh, Holmes?" he said, and his voice was chilling. Soft, sibilant, and smooth, it was like the hissing of a snake. Holmes stirred and moaned. Moriarty bent lower over him, so that their faces were almost touching, and I was reminded of a vampire leaning over his victim. I had the impression that Moriarty would suck Holmes' very life away if I did not stop him.

I was about to say something when I heard another set of footsteps in the hall, and this time the figure which appeared in the doorway was thick, with massive shoulders and a bullet-shaped head.

"Do you have another job for me, Professor?" he said, and I recognized the growling snarl of George Simpson.

Moriarty straightened up and turned to him. "I may, I may, but first

I think you had better wake up our friend here. I have a proposition for him."

"With pleasure," said Simpson, lumbering over to where Holmes lay. I saw his hand raised and heard the sound of fist hitting flesh, and Holmes cried out. I struggled to free myself–I would have killed Simpson then and there if I could have.

"Steady on, you idiot," said Moriarty. "He's no use to us dead, you know."

Simpson grunted and shook Holmes roughly.

"That's enough!" said Moriarty. "I'll take it from here."

Simpson muttered something unintelligible and left the room. Moriarty seated himself stiffly on the floor next to Holmes.

"Holmes," he said, "I have a proposition for you."

"What... is... it?" Holmes said, his voice feeble.

"You tell me where the Star of India is hidden, and I won't kill Dr. Watson here."

There was a silence, and then Holmes spoke. "You... you... can't get away with this, Moriarty."

"Oh, but I can. I shall be safely in India before anyone knows what has happened. This is a very remote area, you know, and no one will hear his screams. Oh, did I mention that I will have him killed very slowly, right before your eyes? Simpson is rather a specialist in such matters, you see, and it would be a pity to waste his talents."

Holmes moved and groaned.

Moriarty leaned over him and whispered softly. "Does it hurt much?"

"Not as much as the pain which is with you all the time, Moriarty," Holmes replied in a weak voice.

Moriarty stood up abruptly. "You're raving," he said scornfully.

"I know, Moriarty... I know all about it... you can't make it go away. Killing us won't alleviate your pain, you know. It's not that easy–"

Moriarty snorted. "Poor Holmes; your mind has been affected. And I thought you were made of stronger stuff."

Just then Freddie Stockton appeared at the door.

"Yes?" Moriarty hissed. "What is it?"

"You're n-n-needed, sir," Stockton stuttered.

Moriarty took a few steps toward the door, and then he turned around. "I'll tell you what. I'll give you exactly ten minutes to think about it, to make your last farewells with the good doctor here, if that's what you should decide. What a touching scene that will be," he continued, moving toward the door. "I shall return in exactly ten minutes," he said, and then he was gone, closing the door behind him.

After he had gone there was a pause, and then Holmes said, "I'm going to give him the information, Watson, even though he will probably have us both killed anyway."

I started to answer, but just then I thought I heard a noise—a faint tapping sound—and I turned to face the window. To my utter astonishment, a small figure squatted on the ground outside the window. A little face peered inside through the glass: it was Jenny! I had an impulse to shout, but I restrained myself.

"Jenny!" I whispered. "Here, Jenny! Can you open the window?"

She made a sign to me and then I heard the sound of a deadbolt being drawn across metal—the sweetest sound I think I have ever heard. In a flash the window was open and the girl crawled nimbly inside, dropping soundlessly to the floor.

"Oh, Jenny, thank God!" I whispered as she began to untie me. "How on earth did you know? I mean, how did you find us?"

"I heard you talking with the gentl'man upstairs at Baker Street," she said as her nimble fingers worked quickly on the ropes which bound me. "I was comin' out of me room to peek, and I sees the other one go upstairs and I says to myself, he's no good, that one. Then I sees them carry you downstairs. I follows them outside real quiet like and I hears what he tells the cab driver. I knew the place right away, o' course, 'cause I knows the river real well, I do, so I comes along here on my own."

"On foot? Alone?"

"It's not so far. I suppose I've gone twice that far on a day's work many a time."

By now I was untied and we were both working to free Holmes, who looked more dead than alive. I helped him to stand up, which he did with difficulty.

"Do you think you can make it out the window, Holmes?" I said.

"I'll try."

Jenny scrambled out first, and then I helped Holmes through and followed last, closing it behind me. As soon as I cleared the window I saw the familiar sight of the Blackfriars Bridge to the west; a sallow setting sun had just sunk under the bridge. The building from which we had just emerged was a dock warehouse of some kind, and lay at the bottom of a muddy embankment leading up to the road. I held Jenny's hand as the three of us scrambled up the bank as fast as Holmes' condition would allow. We scurried up the embankment, hands clawing at the soft clay soil, our fingernails filling with mud. As we reached the top, we heard the chimes of Big Ben tell the hour: six o'clock.

"What time is the ceremony?" Holmes gasped.

"Seven o'clock."

"We must hurry, Watson!"

We dashed across a lot containing other warehouses, and out to the road, where we hailed a cab.

"The Tower of London, as fast as you can!" Holmes cried as we piled in. The cab started up with a jolt, throwing us to the back of the seat. Holmes groaned and held his side.

"Holmes?" I said, but he waved me off.

"I'll be all right, Watson, don't worry," he said as we rattled across the rain-slicked streets.

The avenues were beginning to fill up with people celebrating All Hallows' Eve, and the going became slower as we approached the center of town. Throngs of merrymakers blocked the way. Groups of people were pouring out of pubs in search of merriment and mischief. People dressed as goblins and ghosts were everywhere, carrying candles, flooding the street in a great procession of flickering orange flames. The effect was quite stunning: In the fog, the candles seemed to merge under the gas light into one gigantic fire, a great river of flame moving across the cobblestones. However, we were in no mood to appreciate it.

"This will never do; we'd get there faster on foot," Holmes muttered. Finally, when we reached the crossroad of Victoria and Cannon Streets, Holmes rapped on the roof to signal the driver.

"We'll get out here," he said, giving the man two guineas. "There will be two more for you if you get this girl to 221B Baker Street," he said, indicating Jenny. "Just tell the landlady that Mr. Sherlock Holmes said so."

"I want to come with you!" Jenny cried from inside the cab, but Holmes shook his head.

"You've had enough excitement for one night," he said, and nodded to the cab driver, who flicked his whip and turned the cab around in the direction of Baker Street as we set off on foot through the crowded streets. At the intersection where Great Tower feeds into Byward Street, a gigantic bonfire blazed, and a crowd had gathered to watch a huge puppet of a witch being carried through the streets. Made of sticks and papier mâché, she sat upon her broomstick and hovered over the crowd like a giant black bird, her huge cloth hat flapping in the wind like great dark wings.

"Long live the Queen!" shouted a drunken man as she went by. Suddenly Holmes stopped and grabbed my arm.

"Watson, that's *it!*" he exclaimed.

"What is?"

"Have you heard the expression in chess, 'Give the queen her color?'"

"Yes; it means—"

"The *Black* Queen, Watson! How could I have been so stupid! *I know who the Black Queen is!*"

"Who is it?" I said, but Holmes was already ahead of me. I was amazed at this burst of energy from someone in his condition, but I had known him long enough to realize what he was capable of in times of crisis. I dashed after him, bumping into revelers as I went, hurtling apologies behind me.

Finally we reached the entrance to the Tower. The policeman standing guard stared at us blankly when Holmes announced that he must be allowed inside, but just then Lestrade appeared from inside the gate.

"What is it, Mr. Holmes?" he said. "What's going on?"

"There's no time to explain," said Holmes breathlessly. Lestrade and I followed as he bounded up the steps to the White Tower. The ceremony was being held in the largest of the domed stone chapels, and Lestrade led us to the rear of the crowd which had gathered. Several policemen were at the back of the room with us, standing stiffly at attention, hands at their sides. Holmes' eyes searched the crowd, as if looking for someone. I followed his gaze, but I did not know what he hoped to find.

Up at the altar, among various other dignitaries, sat the queen. To her right was the Prince of Wales, and to his right sat a dignified-looking Indian man dressed in brilliant flowing robes whom I took to be Prince Rabarrath. Behind him stood a darkly handsome, distinguished-looking man also dressed in flowing crimson robes. The man looked familiar, but I could not remember where I had seen him. All eyes were upon the Prince of Wales as he rose to speak, addressing his remarks partly to the crowd and partly to Prince Rabarrath.

Holmes continued to peer at the crowd, as though searching for something or someone in particular.

"What's he looking for?" Lestrade whispered to me, but I shrugged.

"I don't know."

"... and will I hope lead to a renewed sense of commitment between our two great countries," the Prince was saying, his grave dark eyes scanning the crowd as he spoke.

Suddenly Holmes seemed to find whatever it was he was looking for, for his whole body went tense and he leaned forward like a bird dog on a scent.

"... and so, in hopes of promoting this renewed understanding," the Prince continued, "I am pleased to accept formally the very great favor bestowed upon me by His Royal Highness Prince Rabarrath on behalf of his people."

Prince Edward looked back at Prince Rabarrath, who smiled at him. The tall dark man standing behind Rabarrath smiled too, and suddenly I remembered where I had seen him.

"My God, it's the count!" I muttered, turning to Holmes, but he had disappeared, so my remark was addressed to Lestrade instead.

"What?" said Lestrade.

"It's him—the man who stole the Star of India from us!" I said. Now there was no question in my mind that the man standing behind Prince Rabarrath was indeed the same man who had come to Baker Street disguised as the Earl of Huntingdon on that fateful night. I craned my neck to see where Holmes had gone, and was about to make my way through the crowd to look for him. But just then, my eyes were riveted to the stage when I saw what the Prince of Wales held in his hand.

"And now, may I present... the Star of India!" And with that he held up the glittering sapphire so that we could all see it.

"How on earth did he—" I began, but I was interrupted by a commotion in the front of the crowd. I saw the gleam of metal in the light at the same moment I heard the shot. Several people screamed, and others instinctively ducked or began to run for cover. The policemen who had been standing in the back rushed up front to protect the Royal Family and the other dignitaries. Within seconds the queen was surrounded by a phalanx of blue uniforms and whisked offstage. No one appeared to have been hit; the people on the podium looked shaken, but the shot had missed its target. The Prince of Wales stood staring into the crowd. I followed his gaze, and now could see clearly through the crowd who was responsible for the gunshot. Holmes stood, a revolver in one hand, and Miss Violet Merriweather's wrist in the other. Lestrade and I sprang to his assistance.

"I think you'll find the powder marks on her right hand consistent with a recently discharged gun, Inspector," Holmes said as he handed Miss Merriweather over to Lestrade.

"Long live His Majesty Prince Bowdrinth! Down with all traitors to India!" she cried, struggling to free herself.

"Right—thank you, Mr. Holmes," said Lestrade. "Come along, miss; we've got some questions to ask you. Don't worry—everything's under control," he said as he escorted her through the frightened crowd. Holmes and I watched them go and then I looked back at the Prince of Wales. He still stood rooted to the spot, his eyes following Miss Merriweather's retreat. I suddenly saw him not as a prince but as a man deceived in love, and I felt sorry for him as one feels sorry for any man who finds himself betrayed by one he trusted.

Then I remembered the man I had seen standing behind Prince Rabarrath, but both he and the Indian prince had vanished.

"Holmes!" I cried. "Prince Rabarrath's aide—he's not what he appears to be!"

"What do you mean?" said Holmes.

"He's the same man who took the Star of India from me! I'm afraid the prince may be in danger!"

We rushed toward the altar. The room was rapidly clearing as the police escorted people out, trying to maintain as much order as possible.

"There!" cried Holmes, pointing, and I looked just in time to see a flash of crimson disappear through the back entrance.

"Quickly, Watson, after him!" cried Holmes, and set off through what remained of the crowd.

We pushed open a heavy oak door with a tiny barred window; a sign on the door read DANGER—DO NOT OPEN. We found ourselves upon the parapet of the White Tower, where a strong wind was blowing. A gust of wind slammed the heavy door shut behind us as though it were made of paper. The force of the gale nearly took my breath away. I looked at Holmes, who staggered under the powerful blast of air.

"Holmes, look—there!" I cried, shouting to be heard over the wind. There, standing close to edge of the rampart, was our "count." Held close to him was Prince Rabarrath, who struggled to free himself. The wind whipped at their hair and clothing, their robes flying like brightly colored wings around them. Both men saw us at the same moment we saw them, and the prince called out to us in English.

"Help! He's going to kill me!"

"Don't come any closer," said the count, "or I shall be forced to throw him over the edge."

"Don't be foolish," said Holmes. "Give yourself up. There's no escape from here."

The count dragged Prince Rabarrath closer to the edge. Rabarrath was a small man, no match for the tall, athletic count. I took a step forward, but Holmes laid a hand on my arm.

"Wait, Watson! Let us see if we can reason with him," he muttered.

"This will solve nothing, you know," Holmes called to the man.

"Maybe not, but we will accept tyranny no longer!" cried the count. Just at that moment, Prince Rabarrath made a mighty effort and violently pushed his adversary from him—and in the direction of the parapet. As he did so, the count tripped on his own robe and lost his balance. For a moment he teetered on the ledge, his crimson robes blowing in the wind like the feathers of an exotic bird—and then, as we watched in horror, he fell from his perch. His bloodcurdling cry sent shivers up my spine and I turned away. When the sound of his voice died out there was nothing left but the rushing of the wind in our ears. Prince Rabarrath remained seated upon the ground where he had fallen after freeing himself. I walked over to him and offered my hand. Without a word he accepted it, and without a word the three of us left the battlement through the same door we had come out.

Back inside, Prince Rabarrath was immediately surrounded by a group of concerned aides; his absence had caused a momentary panic. They spirited him away, but not before they did he shook our hands warmly.

"Thank you," he said. "I hope I shall have a chance to thank you more formally later." His voice was low and mellow, and his English was excellent, with just a hint of an Eastern flavor in his 'r's.

I turned to Holmes, who was as white as a sheet. He looked as if he were about to collapse. The rush of energy which had filled him earlier had now left, leaving him on the verge of utter prostration. He did not protest when I took him by the arm.

"Come on, Holmes," I said. "Let's go home."

Fourteen

When we arrived at Baker Street, Mycroft was waiting for us in the sitting room.

"Well, Sherlock, so you pulled it off," said Mycroft as we entered. "Good heavens," he exclaimed, rising from his chair, "what has happened to you?"

"It doesn't take a brilliant deduction to figure that out, surely," I muttered as I helped Holmes to the sofa.

"You were quite right, of course; Moriarty rushed in to capture the king, and that proved to be his fatal error," said Mycroft, settling his bulk back into the chair. "You might even say he was castled."

"What does that mean?" I said.

"It is a chess move in which the rook changes places with the king. It is subject to certain restrictions, and certain conditions must be met, but it can be quite useful," answered Mycroft.

"And who is the rook in this case?" I said.

"Why, Sherlock, of course." Mycroft smiled. "And the Black Queen?"

"Miss Merriweather," Holmes said from the sofa.

Mycroft nodded.

"I had my suspicions. What finally gave her away?"

"She used a Hindu word for friend—*dost*—instead of the Bengali word *bandu*, which made me suspicious. I knew many of Rabarrath's enemies are Hindus."

"But how did you know she was to be the assassin?"

"She lived in Blackheath, Mycroft. I had the realization when I saw the figure of a black witch being carried about on the street—and I suddenly remembered the day I escorted Miss Merriweather home to Blackheath."

Mycroft smiled and folded his fat hands over his stomach. "Ah, yes: give the queen her color. Well, where else would the Black Queen come from except Blackheath?"

"Precisely," answered Holmes. "There were of course other things as well. I knew she was lying about her father early on when she claimed he was an Italian opera singer but didn't know the meaning of the Italian word *face*, which is widely used in the opera world to denote the type of voice a singer has. She then claimed her father was a tenor, but when I asked if he had sung the role of Rigoletto she assured me that it was one of his favorites. The role of Rigoletto—surely one of the most famous in the operatic repertoire—is a baritone role."

"There's one thing I don't understand," I said. "How did the prince come by the Star of India if only Holmes knew where it was?"

Mycroft Holmes smiled. "Because he wasn't the only one who knew."

"You knew, then?"

"Yes, indeed. I even suggested it to him."

"Well, where *was* it, then?"

"Why, with the Crown jewels, of course. I suggested hiding it in the last place Moriarty would ever think of looking for it, and the Tower of London seemed to fit the bill. I used my authorization within the government and placed it there myself." Mycroft chuckled. "You should have seen the reaction of the Tower Guard when I told them I was to have access to the Crown jewels... they didn't know what to make of it, but I had a paper with the Royal Seal, so they had to obey."

"I see," I said. "So when it was time for the ceremony–"

"Well, it was a simple matter for the Star to be retrieved; it never had to leave the Tower."

"The White Tower, eh, Sherlock?" Mycroft chuckled. "How very appropriate. That was, of course, the final piece of the puzzle."

Holmes shrugged. "Certainly. Moriarty's instinct for theatricality is second only to mine."

There was a knock on the door and Mrs. Hudson entered. When she saw Holmes she threw her arms up in the air. "Thank God you're safe, sir!" she said. "You don't look so well, though."

"I shall recover, Mrs. Hudson, don't worry," said Holmes.

"Well, at least let me bring you some hot broth." She bustled out of the room, and we all turned to see a small figure standing in the doorway: It was Jenny.

"Come in, Jenny," I said, and she took a few timid steps into the room.

"Ah, here is the real White Queen," said Holmes from where he lay on the sofa.

"Not only that, but she was the Lady in the Lake," I said, rather pleased with myself.

"So she was," said Holmes, "quite right. Do you know what this child did, Mycroft?"

Mycroft shook his head. Jenny stood there shyly while Holmes and I told him of our capture and rescue. When we were finished, Jenny tiptoed over to Holmes and kissed him on the forehead.

"What was that for?" he asked, embarrassed.

"Mrs. Hudson said it would make you get better faster," she answered. Mycroft and I laughed.

"And if that doesn't do it, this will," said Mrs. Hudson from the doorway where she stood with a steaming bowl of hot soup. Just then Inspector Lestrade appeared behind Mrs. Hudson, who turned and saw him.

"Oh, begging your pardon, Inspector," she said; "I was just about to tell Mr. Holmes you were here." She placed the soup on the coffee table and turned to me. "Now you be sure that he has some of that, Dr. Watson," she said. "Come along, dearie, let's go make some tea for the gentlemen," she said to Jenny, who got up obediently and followed her out of the room.

"Please come in, inspector," I said, rising from my chair.

"Thank you," said Lestrade, entering the room.

"Please sit down," I said, pulling up a chair for him.

"'Ta very much. Good evening, Mr. Holmes," he said to Mycroft.

"Good evening, Inspector. I understand it's been a busy one for you."

"You might say that, although thanks to Mr. Holmes here I think we've got the situation under control for now. You were right," he said to Holmes. "Miss Merriweather, as she called herself, was a member of Prince Bowdrinth's gang ever since her brother was killed in a skirmish by one of Rabarrath's people. Her real name is Sree Malthi; she was working for Bowdrinth's people all along, feeding them information, and then when it looked like their scheme was going to fail, they sent her to kill the Prince."

"So *was* Moriarty involved in the assassination plot?" I said.

Lestrade shrugged. "No one knows—he's disappeared. I have sent some lads out to round up some of his men, but they have a habit of disappearing too, it seems."

Mycroft got up and sat in Holmes' chair by the fire. "Oh, he was involved—I would bet money on it. And, as my brother can tell you, I am not a gambling man."

Holmes turned over onto his side and grimaced. "He will probably drop out of sight for a while until things cool down, but you will hear from him again, Inspector—mark my words."

Lestrade nodded. "I've no doubt you're right, Mr. Holmes."

"Speaking of dropping out of sight, Sherlock, what *did* happen at the Bar of Gold opium den?" said Mycroft.

"I learned several interesting things before my identity was discovered. Your man Hazelton was betrayed, Lestrade. I found that out for certain at the Bar of Gold—though I had suspected as much. Then I was discovered, captured, and taken to Moriarty, who hoped he could persuade me to give up the location of the jewel."

"And he very nearly succeeded," I said. "And the count— who was he?"

"Oh, the one who fell from the Tower? Nasty affair, that," said Lestrade.

"He was undoubtedly one of Bowdrinth's people too," said Mycroft. "Moriarty' s web stretches farther than we'll probably ever know. Even I haven't yet fathomed the extent of his influence."

"Wait, there's something I don't understand," I interjected. "Miss Merriweather presumably could have killed Prince Edward at any time while she was his mistress—"

"Oh, but that was a last resort," said Mycroft Holmes. "And even so, it had to look like a political act, not the revenge of a spurned lover."

"Something else bothers me," said Lestrade. "Why did she give Mr. Holmes the Star of India?"

"Part of Moriarty's plan was to draw my brother in and then destroy him," said Mycroft. "He probably had three or four plans for getting the jewel back. If Miss Merriweather herself surrendered the jewel, who would think to suspect her? And then she stayed in close contact, hoping to gather information as to how things were proceeding from our side. However, she failed to reckon with my brother's notorious distrust of women—didn't she, Sherlock?"

Holmes waved his hand as if dismissing the thought. "I should have mistrusted anybody under the circumstances, I think, though I did think she played the part of the female in distress rather heavily."

"Well, she took me in, and I'm not ashamed to admit it," I said.

Holmes smiled. "Well, I have always said the ladies were your department, Watson, but you made the mistake of letting your heart override your head."

I felt my face redden as Lestrade and Mycroft looked at me. It was a weakness in my character, perhaps, but I was still unable to reconcile Miss Merriweather's actions with her beautiful face and figure. That a woman could look like such an angel and be so devious was difficult to comprehend. I wondered if even her attraction to Holmes had been an act to throw him off the scent, but somehow I didn't think so; she was clever enough to know of his famous distrust of women. No, I believed still that her reaction to him may have been the one real thing about her.

"Never mind, Dr. Watson," Lestrade said. "We all have our momentary lapses of judgment."

"Speaking of which, have you plugged your leak yet, Lestrade?" said Holmes.

Lestrade looked down at the floor and rubbed his hands together nervously. "Yes, I did, Mr. Holmes."

"It was Morgan?"

Lestrade nodded. "Yes. You were right; he had been spying on me using the parrot. When I was out he'd write down whatever the bird said and then give it to Moriarty. We caught him red-handed, though, once you told me what to look for." Lestrade walked over to the window and looked out onto the street below, where the sound of horses' hooves on cobblestone mingled with the patter of rain on the windowpanes. "I suppose I'll have to get rid of Ban—get rid of the bird now," he said in a tight voice.

"Oh, I don't see why you shouldn't keep him, Lestrade," I said. "You can always take him home."

"Yeah, I guess I could at that," Lestrade said, brightening. "The thing is… well, he's sort of gotten used to life around the Yard—I mean, I think he likes it there."

Mycroft Holmes rolled his eyes and rose from his chair. He stood with his broad back to the fire, rocking back and forth on his heels.

"I'm sure you'll think of something, Lestrade," I said kindly.

"Right; of course," Lestrade said, suddenly aware that we were all looking at him. "Well, I suppose I'll be on my way," he said, rising from his chair just as Mrs. Hudson entered with a tray of tea. Jenny followed behind her with a plate of sandwiches and butterscotch biscuits.

"Don't leave yet, Inspector," she said, "I've just made tea."

Both Mycroft Holmes and Lestrade looked considerably more cheerful at the sight of the food, and I had to admit I was rather famished myself.

It was late before everyone left, and only then would Holmes allow me to attend to his injuries.

"Human nature is really beyond all comprehension," he said as I applied iodine to his forehead. "Four men dead, the prince nearly shot—and over what? A rock. Corundum, a mineral with a six-sided crystalline structure. And for this men plot and fight and kill each other…" He sighed and shook his head.

"Hold still, please," I said. "This was about more than just the Star of India, you know, Holmes," I added as I wound a dressing round his head.

"Oh, yes, no doubt the future of India is important... and there are certainly changes coming, perhaps not in our lifetime, but soon enough. Still, Watson, why must people continually grasp and grab and harm one another, when life is so short?"

"So that you have something to do," I said, "to keep you from dying of boredom or overdosing on cocaine."

Holmes looked at me and frowned.

"Really, Watson, that is unworthy of you. Is that really what you think of me?"

I shrugged. "I am afraid it is what you think of yourself."

"Well, perhaps you are right," he said thoughtfully, and then he smiled. "I wonder what your friend Mr. Freud would have to say on the matter?"

"I really am more interested at the moment on what Mrs. Hudson has for us in the kitchen," I said, closing up my doctor's kit. "I'm starving." It had been hours since our tea and sandwiches.

"Why don't you go find out?"

And so I did—I tiptoed downstairs so as not to wake Mrs. Hudson or Jenny, and to my delight there was a cold rack of lamb and some pudding in the icebox. I made a tray up and brought it upstairs.

"Look, Holmes, what I found!" I said, opening the door to the sitting room, but there was no reply—he was already asleep. I stood over him for a few moments and watched him sleep. I could only hope he was, for a time at least, safe from the nightmares which haunted him.

Epilogue

"Well Watson," Holmes said some nights later, as we sat down to the roast which Mrs. Hudson had prepared for our dinner, "how are you going to write this one up?"

"I don't know," I said, pouring myself a glass of Bordeaux. "Now that I look back on everything that happened, I can't help wondering if anyone would believe it. Besides, I fear your reputation might suffer if it became known that you were saved by a ten-year-old girl."

Holmes smiled. "How thoughtful of you. How is Jenny getting along in Cornwall, by the way?"

"Oh, famously. She has become quite a pet of the village, it seems. Mrs. Hudson says she wants to come to London for a visit soon."

Jenny had gone to live with Flora Campbell, Mrs. Hudson's sister. Both of the sisters doted on her, and she, in turn, was flourishing in the healthy country air of the seaside.

"Oh, by the way, I received this by messenger today. I thought you might like to see it," he said, and handed me a cream-colored envelope across the table. When I saw the coat of arms emblazoned on the envelope I looked at Holmes.

"Read it," he said.

I removed the card from its envelope with trembling hands. The writing, elegant if a little unsteady with age, read, "We are most grateful for your services. Your country owes you its gratitude.–V.R."

I put the card down and stared at Holmes, who was unable to contain his amusement at my reaction.

"Not bad, eh, Watson?"

"Perhaps I am a stodgy old traditionalist, but really, Holmes, even you must be a *little* impressed. A handwritten note from–"

"From the White Queen, Watson... and so her kingdom has been preserved–for a time." He rose from the table and looked out onto the kaleidoscope of life just outside our window. "But I wonder, Watson, I wonder... change is the only constant in this little world of ours, and there are changes coming, changes which any one man will be unable to prevent."

He stood there for a moment, his sharp profile silhouetted in the gaslight, and then he turned back to me. "Well, Watson, what do you say to a trip to the Royal Albert? I see that Wilma Norman-Neruda is playing Mozart. We have just enough time to purchase tickets."

"Very well," I replied, "but you must promise me that we won't buy a seat next to any mysterious young women."

"Oh, come, Watson, where's your sense of adventure?"

"I've had enough adventure for a while–and so have you."

"Perhaps you're right... maybe it's time to retire from this hazardous line of work. Perhaps from now on I shall stick to reading your accounts of my exploits from the safety of my armchair. After all, what is fame, Watson? I think it's about time that I retire into a grateful obscurity."

I looked out of the window at the gathering twilight which wrapped itself around the lampposts like a shroud. Moriarty still lived; London would always be London, and Sherlock Holmes... well, suffice it to say that some things never change. I have no great opinion of my literary gifts, and yet even I dare to hope that so long as cab wheels clatter upon cobblestones, so long as yellow fogs settle early upon rain-slicked streets; in short, as long as the yearning for adventure throbs in the hearts of men, somewhere there will always be someone to thrill to the words: "Watson, come quickly—the game is afoot!"

Acknowledgments

First and foremost, deepest gratitude to my friend and colleague Marvin Kaye, without whom this book never would have been written. Thanks also to my editor at St Martin's, Keith Kahla, whose unerring eye was invaluable during the rewriting process; to Susan Ginsburg and John Hodgman at Writers House for all their hard work; to Anthony Moore for his support in discussions over endless cups of tea; to Robert Murphy for lending me his guidebooks of London; to Chris Buggé for introducing me to the wonders of the Cornish coastline, and to Latif Kahn and the rest of my friends at Royal India Cuisine for keeping my spirits up with a continuous supply of both information and chicken tandoori. Finally, thanks to Sir Arthur Conan Doyle, whose immortal creation has fired the imaginations of so many who came after him; I am honored to tread in his footsteps.

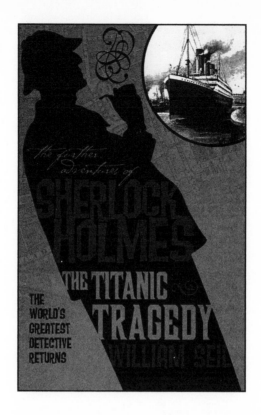

THE FURTHER ADVENTURES
OF Sherlock Holmes
THE TITANIC TRAGEDY

William Seil

Sherlock Holmes and Dr. Watson board the Titanic in 1912, where Holmes is
to carry out a secret government mission. Soon after departure, highly important
submarine plans for the U.S. Navy are stolen. Holmes and Watson work through a
list of suspects which includes Colonel James Moriarty, brother to the late Professor
Moriarty—will they find the culprit before tragedy strikes?

ISBN: 9780857687104

AVAILABLE MARCH 2012

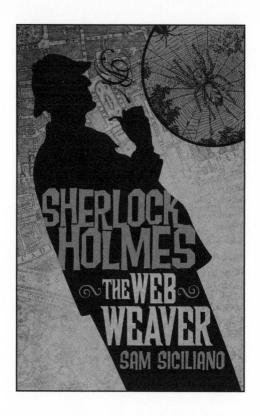

THE FURTHER ADVENTURES
OF SHERLOCK HOLMES

THE WEB WEAVER

Sam Siciliano

A mysterious gypsy places a cruel curse on the guests at a ball. When a series of terrible misfortunes affect those who attended the ball, Mr. Donald Wheelwight engages Sherlock Holmes to find out what really happened that night. With the help of his cousin Dr. Henry Vernier and his wife Michelle, Holmes endeavors to save Wheelwright and his beautiful wife Violet from the devastating curse.

ISBN: 9780857686985

AVAILABLE JANUARY 2012

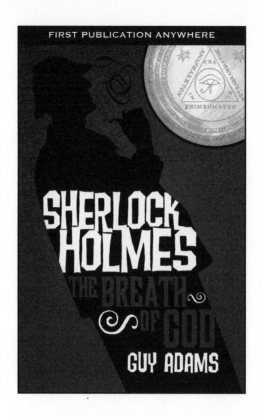

THE FURTHER ADVENTURES
OF SHERLOCK HOLMES

THE BREATH OF GOD

Guy Adams

A body is found crushed to death in the London snow. There are no footprints anywhere near. It is almost as if the man was killed by the air itself. This is the first in a series of attacks that sees a handful of London's most prominent occultists murdered. While pursuing the case, Holmes and Watson have to travel to Scotland to meet with the one person they have been told can help: Aleister Crowley.
ISBN: 9780857682826

AVAILABLE SEPTEMBER 2011

THE FURTHER ADVENTURES
OF SHERLOCK HOLMES

THE PEERLESS PEER

Philip José Farmer

During the Second World War, Mycroft Holmes dispatches his brother Sherlock
and Dr. Watson to recover a stolen formula. During their perilous journey, they
are captured by a German zeppelin. Subsequently forced to abandon ship, the
pair parachute into the dark African jungle where they encounter the lord of the
jungle himself...

ISBN: 9780857681201

AVAILABLE NOW!

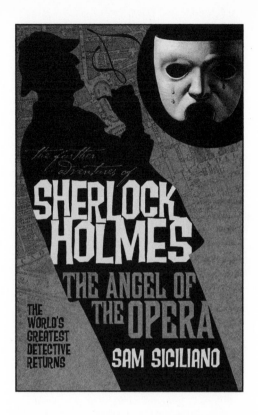

THE FURTHER ADVENTURES
OF SHERLOCK HOLMES

THE ANGEL OF THE OPERA

Sam Siciliano

Paris 1890: Sherlock Holmes is called across the English Channel to the famous
Opera House, where he is challenged to discover the true motivations and secrets of
the notorious Phantom who rules its depths with passion and defiance.

ISBN: 9781848568617

AVAILABLE NOW!

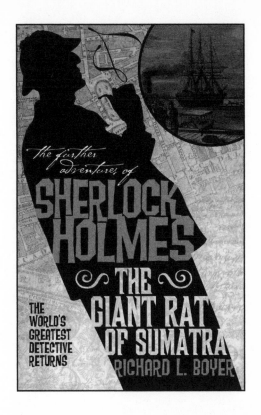

THE FURTHER ADVENTURES
OF SHERLOCK HOLMES

THE GIANT RAT OF SUMATRA

Richard L. Boyer

For many years, Dr. Watson kept the tale of The Giant Rat of Sumatra a secret.
However, before he died, he arranged that the strange story of the giant rat should
be held in the vaults of a London bank until all the protagonists were dead...
ISBN: 9781848568600

AVAILABLE NOW!

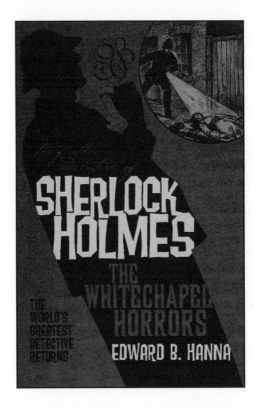

THE FURTHER ADVENTURES
OF SHERLOCK HOLMES

DR. JEKYLL AND MR. HOLMES

Loren D. Estleman

When Sir Danvers Carew is brutally murdered, the Queen herself calls on
Sherlock Holmes to investigate. In the course of his enquiries, the esteemed
detective is struck by the strange link between the highly respectable Dr.
Henry Jekyll and the immoral, debauched Edward Hyde...
ISBN: 9781848567474

AVAILABLE NOW!

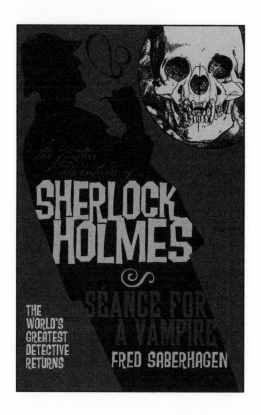

THE FURTHER ADVENTURES
OF SHERLOCK HOLMES
SÉANCE FOR A VAMPIRE

Fred Saberhagen

Wealthy British aristocrat Ambrose Altamont hires Sherlock Holmes
to expose two suspect psychics. During the ensuing séance, Altamont's
deceased daughter reappears as a vampire–and Holmes vanishes. Watson
has no choice but to summon the only one who might be able to help–
Holmes' vampire cousin, Prince Dracula.
ISBN: 9781848566774

AVAILABLE NOW!

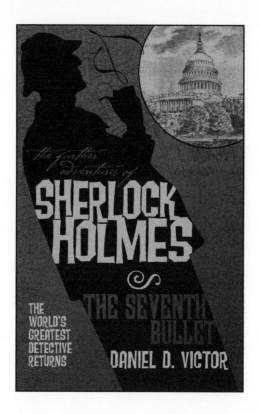

THE FURTHER ADVENTURES
OF SHERLOCK HOLMES

THE SEVENTH BULLET

Daniel D. Victor

Sherlock Holmes and Dr. Watson travel to New York City to
investigate the assassination of true-life muckraker and author
David Graham Phillips. They soon find themselves caught in a
web of deceit, violence and political intrigue, which only the great
Sherlock Holmes can unravel.

ISBN: 9781848566767

AVAILABLE NOW!

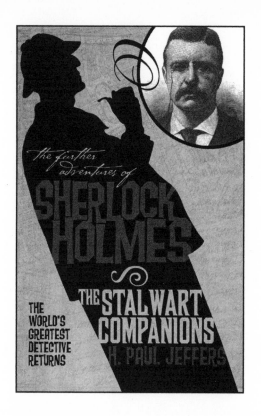

THE FURTHER ADVENTURES
OF SHERLOCK HOLMES

THE STALWART COMPANIONS

H. Paul Jeffers

Written by future President Theodore Roosevelt long before The
Great Detective's first encounter with Dr. Watson, Holmes visits
America to solve a most violent and despicable crime. A crime that
was to prove the most taxing of his brilliant career.
ISBN: 9781848565098

AVAILABLE NOW!

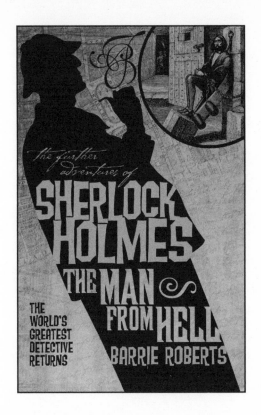

THE FURTHER ADVENTURES
OF SHERLOCK HOLMES
THE WAR OF THE WORLDS

Manley W. Wellman & Wade Wellman

Sherlock Holmes, Professor Challenger and Dr. Watson meet
their match when the streets of London are left decimated by
a prolonged alien attack. Who could be responsible for such
destruction? Sherlock Holmes is about to find out...
ISBN: 9781848564916

AVAILABLE NOW!